From East to West

Critical Perspectives on English and American Literature, Communication and Culture

Volume 27

Edited by

María José Álvarez-Faedo
Andrew Monnickendam
Beatriz Penas-Ibáñez

PETER LANG

Bern · Berlin · Bruxelles · New York · Oxford

Martin Simonson &
Jon Alkorta Martiartu

From East to West

The Portrayal of Nature in British Fantasy and its
Projection in Ursula K. Le Guin's Western
American *Earthsea*

PETER LANG

Bern · Berlin · Bruxelles · New York · Oxford

Bibliographic Information published by the Deutsche Nationalbibliothek

The Deutsche Nationalbibliothek lists this publication in the Deutsche Nationalbibliografie; detailed bibliographic data is available in the internet at http://dnb.d-nb.de.

Library of Congress Cataloging-in-Publication Data
A CIP catalog record for this book has been applied for at the Library of Congress.

This essay has been completed under the auspices of the research group REWEST, funded by the Basque Government (IT-1026-16), and by the research Project "NEW WESTS: EL OESTE AMERICANO EN LA LITERATURA, EL CINE Y LA CULTURA DEL SIGLO XXI: UN ENFOQUE TRANSNACIONAL Y TRANSDISCIPLINAR" (Ministerio de Ciencia, Innovación y Universidades: PGC2018-094659-B-C2).

ISSN 1662-2383 • ISBN 978-3-0343-4250-6 (Print)
E-ISBN 978-3-0343-4327-5 (E-PDF) • E-ISBN 978-3-0343-4328-2 (EPUB)
E-ISBN 978-3-0343-4329-9 (MOBI) • DOI 10.3726/b18375

This publication has been peer reviewed.

© Peter Lang Group AG
International Academic Publishers
Bern 2021
All rights reserved.

www.peterlang.com

This essay has been completed under the auspices of the research group REWEST, funded by the Basque Government (IT-1026-16), and by the research Project "NEW WESTS: EL OESTE AMERICANO EN LA LITERATURA, EL CINE Y LA CULTURA DEL SIGLO XXI: UN ENFOQUE TRANSNACIONAL Y TRANSDISCIPLINAR" (Ministerio de Ciencia, Innovación y Universidades: PGC2018-094659-B-C2)

This book is for David Rio and Amaia Ibarraran, in token of their trust and patience. My thanks also go to the anonymous reviewers of the manuscript, whose insightful comments greatly improved the text.

Martin

To Martin and Raúl for giving me the chance to start this journey.
To my family and Maialen for their patience and support.

Jon

Table of Contents

Introduction

The powers of nature have been a defining feature of all civilizations and human identity throughout history, and will inevitably remain one until anything akin to a post-human civilization has been established—if such a regrettable state of affairs should ever occur. As a consequence, myths and other types of narratives aiming to make sense of the world and give it meaning, have hinged upon the relationship between human beings and nature to a very great extent; from the earliest known nature-myths to modern science fiction dealing with the tensions between earthly bonds and digital reality.

In literature dealing with the fantastic, the natural world has been one of the central characters from the beginning. It has consistently displayed a fascination with natural phenomena and our varying interpretations of them, acting as a threshold for liminal experiences of reality, or serving as potent metaphors for different aspects of the human condition in fantastic guises. The natural world has been a force to contend or blend with, a repository of mystery or a source of horror; its portrayal has consistently reflected the particular preoccupations of the age in which the works were written. In epic literature, it was the abode of monsters of the mind, but also a guarantor of bliss and harmony. In the Middle Ages, nature was frequently given a symbolic treatment that reflected the concerns of an aristocratic society obsessed with courtly love and manners, while in the eighteenth century, nature in the Gothic novel centered on the sublime and embodied a subversive aesthetic that questioned the prevailing Enlightened notions of order, symmetry and harmony, centering instead on the dark and threatening aspects of the natural world.

The Romantic period became a turning point in the fantastic portrayal of nature. Influenced both by pseudo-medieval aesthetics and the Gothic fascination with how external, sublime landscapes reflected the inner turmoil and hidden recesses of the human mind, Romantic writers initiated a conscious exploration of how the forces of nature were connected to a higher reality, and how we could access both by means of the human imagination, conceived of as the "soul". As a consequence, the literary portrayal of nature became increasingly imaginative, and the nineteenth century saw the rise of various modes of imaginative fiction, ranging from original fairy tales to tales of horror and pseudo-medieval prose romances, that coalesced into the emergence of modern fantasy in the early years of the twentieth century. In the Edwardian period, nature and the countryside were seen as the true repository of autochthonous culture, myth, and literature, overtly threatened by a growing sense of unease concerning Britain's hegemonic role in the world, and modern Englishmen, frequently based in cities, developed a strong nostalgia. English identity was seen as fundamentally connected to the country, not the city. The country and nature became invested with a decidedly mystic aura, and interpreted both as an ancient home, and as something ostensibly foreign to the modern experience. This dichotomy allowed for transcendental explorations of a liminal space, where modern Englishmen were exposed to a timeless, mythic past. That this exploration occurred simultaneously in genres as varied as children's literature and horror fiction, testifies to its strength in the period.

The Great War only served to enhance the British obsession with nature—enhanced, as Fussell rightly holds, by a long tradition of pastoral poetry which had dominated the national literature, and also by the fact that England had been exposed so early to the industrial revolution that by the time we reach the twentieth century, a nostalgia for the countryside had already been deeply ingrained in the cultural core for many generations. Add to this an Empire with many hundreds of thousands of Englishmen working in the administration of the colonies, and the ingredients for a powerful nostalgia for the English countryside, pictured as a kind of paradise which was antithetical both to colonial life and later to the infernal scenery of the trenches, and we have a fertile ground for further development of a type of fantasy literature which held on even tighter to the rural world.

Not in vain, it was a man born in South Africa that would establish the basic parameters for epic fantasy in the twentieth century. As I have argued elsewhere, in J.R.R. Tolkien's *The Lord of the Rings* (1954–55) there is a mélange of ancient and modern modes of narrative discourse, and Middle-earth acts as an extended chronotope that hosts the different traditions simultaneously, making room for a dialogue between them deprived of the ironic clashes that were so frequent in the modernist literature that belonged to the mode of what Northrop Frye has labelled "ironic myth". In doing so, Tolkien brought into his vast narrative the corresponding world-visions of the ancient and more recent societies in which a very unmodern discourse made sense, and with them their respective attitudes and appreciations of the natural world.

Ursula K. Le Guin's *Earthsea* books were written in the genre of epic fantasy that Tolkien was so instrumental in establishing. However, Le Guin was two generations younger than Tolkien, she was a woman, and—most importantly—she grew up and came to her own as a writer in the American West; a very different cultural, natural and social context compared to Tolkien's. For these reasons, if we wish to properly assess the role of nature in Le Guin's work, we need to look at two different contexts: the Tolkienian mode of fantasy, in turn heavily informed by ancient and more recent modes of narrative discourse, and Le Guin's own Western American context. It is our aim in this book to discuss the "classic" portrayals of nature in a very long and fertile British literary tradition of the fantastic, and compare them with Le Guin's vision of nature in her *Earthsea* books, in order to see how the latter's literature simultaneously articulates a perpetuation and a deviation from the received tradition. By doing so, we will hopefully be able to disclose the structural and thematic strength of the generic tendrils, but also to show the impact of a specific cultural, historical and natural context on Le Guin's portrayal of nature.

While the bulk of previous research on Le Guin's fiction has centred on her science-fiction output, among the comprehensive studies which do take her fantasy literature into account, Harold Bloom's 1986 anthology of essays *Ursula K. Le Guin* includes three essays that were useful to us at an early stage in our research. "The Good Witch of the West" by Robert Scholes, "The Magic Art and the Evolution of Words: The Earthsea Trilogy" by Tom Shippey, and George Slusser's "The Earthsea Trilogy" helped us to situate Le Guin's attitudes towards Christianity, her use of language in relation to magic, and the concept of the equilibrium which underlies the literary fashioning of Earthsea.

Individual full-length studies concerning the importance of language in Le Guin's created universe, which is essential for the existence and life of Earthsea, include Deirdre Byrne PhD dissertation "Selves and Others: The Politics of Difference in the Writings of Ursula Kroeber Le Guin" (1995), in which she addresses the implications of language and naming, while Laura Comoletti and Michael Drout focus on the relationship between language and magic and its multilayered consequences in their co-authored article "How They Do Things with Words: Language, Power, Gender, and the Priestly Wizards of Ursula K. Le Guin's Earthsea Books" (2001). Both works helped us determine more closely the relationship between language and world-making in Earthsea.

Other important works of reference which have been of use to us in the present study include those of Warren Rochelle concerning the presence of American Transcendentalist ideals in Le Guin's fantasy literature. In *Communities of the Heart. The Rhetoric of Myth in the Fiction of Ursula K. Le Guin* (2001), Rochelle describes the type of universe that Le Guin depicts in Earthsea and how humans inhabit it, but even more essential to us was "The Emersonian Choice: Connections Between Dragons and Humans in Le Guin's Earthsea Cycle" (2006), since it provided a starting point for our own study of the dragons and their relationship with identity and ecology in Earthsea. Holly Littlefield's analysis of the depiction of women and their social role in Earthsea, "Unlearning Patriarchy: Ursula Le Guin's Feminist Consciousness in The Tombs of Atuan and Tehanu" (1995), has also been an important inspiration (although our point of view concerning the question of female characters does not completely align with Littlefield's).

Last, some words should be devoted to the studies which make a conscious use of ecocriticism, or center on the portrayal of nature in Earthsea. Here, we should mention John Crow and Richard Erlich's "Words of Binding: Patterns of Integration in the Earthsea Trilogy" (1979), Tonya Payne's PhD dissertation "'A Heart That Watches and Receives': Ursula Le Guin and the American Nature-Writing Tradition" (1999), and Shu Fen Tsai's "Le Guin's Earthsea Cycle: An Ecological Fable of 'Healing Wounds'" (2003). These studies have mainly contributed with ideas about how Earthsea functions as a natural universe—in line with Rochelle's work—and what it can teach us about our own relationship with the real natural world.

While all the aforementioned works have helped us determine Le Guin's portrayal of nature in her Earthsea saga more closely, very few of them apply their findings to the broader picture of Earthsea as a universe where nature is placed at the very core. In light of this, we have selected from and blended these heterogeneous pieces of research to compose our ecocritical point of departure, which is more comprehensive and aims to determine how nature has been depicted in the world of Earthsea. It thus differs from previous research in that we have aimed to convey a more detailed and complete picture of the factors that make Earthsea what it is, and their impact on the relationship between nature and humans, where each affects—and is in turn affected by—the other. This could only have been done because we had the advantage, compared to most of the previous research, of having had access to *all* of the tales that make up this saga (the last of which was published in 2017).

In order to convey this more comprehensive approach to Earthsea properly, the first part of the book is made up of three chapters looking at the background of the literary genre in which Le Guin's works are situated, epic fantasy, and its changing relationship with nature. Modern epic fantasy was a predominantly British affair up to the end of the nineteenth century, so it is to British literature we turn in the first chapter, in search of key examples taken from different literary traditions of the British past, of how the natural world has been represented in literature from the fantastic "canon". While it is true that this national tradition is much informed by other literatures—notably the works of Classical Antiquity, French medieval romances and German original fairy tales—British literature is characterized by an extraordinary capacity to absorb and transform received modes of discourse into a national body of literature. The different examples serve to show us how the varying modes have preserved one central strand in their representation of nature: that of the natural world as a liminal area, a place in which characters and readers are forced to negotiate their own role on the threshold of a mythic, supernatural reality.

In the second chapter, we look at how Victorian fin-de-siècle anxieties warp into Edwardian narratives centering on a very modern reassessment of the countryside, and how a number of fantastic expressions of nature emerged as a result. This literary and cultural milieu informed the writings of J.R.R. Tolkien and H.P. Lovecraft, who grew up on the British literature produced in these years (albeit on different sides of the Atlantic), and their own renderings would have an enormous impact on the North American writers of science fiction, horror and fantasy, among them Le Guin.

J.R.R. Tolkien is arguably the single most important writer in the emergence of modern epic fantasy, and Le Guin ackowledged his influence on her own writing. In relation to the present study, after the First World War, it was Tolkien, in particular, who synthesized the Edwardian explorations of the countryside and produced his own, highly original vision of the preceding literary traditions. This is the subject of chapter 3, which ends with a section that describes Tolkien's vision of the mythical West, largely based on ancient Celtic and Norse legends.

This serves to set off the first part of the central chapter of this study, which provides an outline of the specifically Western American conditions that affected Le Guin, and that would find their way into the fabric of her *Earthsea* tales, in which Tolkien's vision of a mythic West is redefined and explored much more extensively. From this starting point, we move on to a detailed study of a central being in the universe of Earthsea: the dragons. This analysis will allow us to see just how closely related these beings are to nature in Le Guin's work, apart from the implications of their presence in the West. We will then move on to take a look at the depiction of nature in Le Guin's *Earthsea* saga, focusing on two central areas. First, we will examine the genesis of the fictional world and its implications for nature, whose bonds with humanity become extremely deteriorated over time, eventually leading to a complete alienation of humans from the ecosystem. Second, we will analyse two key protagonists' diverse responses to nature in a world that has been shaped by humanity's greed for domination.

It is by now a commonplace to stress the need to redefine our relationship with the natural world in order to create a more balanced relationship with our environment, and creative and artistic examples such as Le Guin's show that it is possible to break free from inherited ways of looking at the world—in this case the literary genre she works in, and the natural world—without severing all our ties to them. There are parts of the tradition that are well worth saving, but they have to be "naturally" integrated into the fabric of our everyday life and culture. Fantasy literature is one important vehicle for such projects, and Le Guin's work is an astonishingly suggestive example of how it can be done.

I The Discourse of Nature in British Imaginative Literature: From the Middle Ages to the Early Twentieth Century

It is the purpose of this chapter to provide some background on how nature has been portrayed in British literature throughout the ages. It is necessary to do so, because Le Guin's *Earthsea* cycle belongs to a genre commonly known as epic fantasy; a literary mode established mainly by J.R.R. Tolkien in works like *The Lord of the Rings*, which set the standards for subsequent fantasy literature written in this field. As I have argued elsewhere (Simonson 2008), one of the traits of this genre is that it puts different historical narrative traditions in dialogue on a simultaneous level, so the first step is to provide an outline of how nature has been portrayed in some salient examples taken from the Western canon, with which both Tolkien and Le Guin were intimately familiar. We shall then concentrate in some detail on the Edwardian period, a post-Romantic moment in history in which the foundations of modern fantasy were laid, and whose literary expression of nature affected J.R.R. Tolkien, who grew up in this period and would himself be instrumental in creating the genre in which Le Guin would later write *Earthsea*.

The expression of nature in the Anglo-Saxon period

English literature is said to begin with *Beowulf*, a work of narrative verse written in Old English at some point in the 8th century. *Beowulf* is indebted to age-old myths and other preceding narrative genres, such as heroic poetry and the folktale—but above all to the epic tradition of Classical Antiquity, which blend all three. Epic literature came into being when heroic poetry was expanded with inquiries and digressions concerning issues fundamental to the human condition (Hainsworth 5).

Frequently, this involved reaching out to mythic paradigms, which usually prompted the intervention of supernatural elements of different kinds in the natural world. At the same time, the narratives were endowed with a greater coherence in their presentation of the world, which was made comprehensive enough to include not only the world of men, but also the subterranean and divine dimensions. The semi-primordial temporal framework enabled the poets to portray supernatural characters and events without yielding completely to the folktale's more frivolous marvels, since the glorious past was conceived of as a time when the gods would frequently interact with elected humans.

The natural world in these works is given a great deal of solidity, in spite of its frequently fantastic character. The enchanted archipelago in the Odyssey or the underworld in the Aeneid, to give two examples, are presented as real places, which human heroes of flesh and blood can enter and interact with. In the case of the anonymously written epic poem *Beowulf,* which was composed at some point in the 8th century, probably in the region of Northumbria or Mercia, in the northeast of what we today know as England (Alexander 9–12), we are dealing with an epic narrative that involves several fantastic scenes and places. The story as such is about the eponymous Beowulf, a young hero from Gautland (in the south of present-day Sweden) who travels over the sea to King Hrothgar's court in Denmark to help him get rid of the bothersome Grendel, a monster that has been attacking the royal hall of Heoroth, humiliating the king and making the Danes' lives miserable. After chasing off Grendel and chopping off the monster's arm, Beowulf follows its footprints to a lake, at the bottom of which he dispatches Grendel's mother in her underwater den. A monster dwelling in a cave in the depths of a lake would obviously present serious problems to anyone but an semi-divine hero. Luckily, this is the case of Beowulf, whose supernatural origins are never fully disclosed but instead implied by his superhuman strength. In the remote mere, our epic hero is challenged not only with the task of slaying monsters; he also has to take on a natural environment with clear fantastic tinges that will test his strength, endurance and skill.

The descriptions of the lugubrious lake are succinct and to the point, and make it clear that it will be no easy task to overcome the natural obstacles: "On a sudden he came upon the mountain trees leaning over the hoar rock, a joyless forest. Bloodstained and troubled water loomed beneath" (Tolkien, Beowulf 54). The emphasis in the description falls upon the intended emotions conveyed by the landscape: it is a sad, lonely, wild and positively hostile place, full of mortal danger. The poem continues: "they saw about the water many of the serpent kind, strange dragons of the sea, ranging the flood, and demons of the deep lying upon the jutting slopes, even such as in the middle hours watch for those journeying anxious upon the sailing paths, serpents and beasts untamed" (Tolkien, Beowulf 54).

Apart from the tangible references to sea-monsters of previous epic narratives, such as Ulysses' famous adventures, it is worthy of note that the place itself serves as a marker of boundaries, a threshold which justifies the presence of all sorts of supernatural horrors. While darkness and night cloak the ostensibly supernatural interventions of the monster Grendel (and later the attack of the ogre's mother, who suddenly appears in the civilized Heoroth to slay King Hrothgar's best men), here it is the landscape itself that marks the passage to a realm where ordinary rules of realism cease to apply. The "joyless forest", the "hoar rock" and the "bloodstained and troubled water" are all markers of liminality which simultaneously emphasize and legitimate the presence of the supernatural in a type of narrative which is otherwise heavily focused on celebrating heroic exploits. However, for the very same reason that mythic narratives are presented as true, in epic narratives the fantastic elements are also meant to be taken literally; if not, the heroic exploits would cease to be relevant and admirable. Descriptions of landscape and nature become a tool of the epic poets to lead the audience on imaginative paths into a borderland where distinctions between the real and the fantastic become blurred, but in which the heroes remain "real" men, in spite of their superhuman heroic stature and powers. This is no small poetic feat in itself, given that Beowulf plunges into the mere where

> a long hour of the day it was before he could descry the level floor. Straightway that creature that with cruel lust, ravenous and grim, had a hundred seasons held the watery realm, perceived that there from on high some man was come to espy the dwelling of inhuman things ... Then that she-wolf of the waves to the sea-bottom coming bore the mail-clad prince unto her own abode. (Tolkien, Beowulf 56)

In spite of the amount of time spent underwater, Beowulf's inability to unsheathe his sword, and the constant attacks of all manner of strange sea-beasts and monsters who "with fell tusks at his hauberk tore", Beowulf not only survives the seemingly impossible ordeal, but once dragged into the monster's underwater den he rapidly recovers and slays Grendel's mother. The use of a third-person omniscient perspective lends an appearance of objectivity to the narrative, but the real measure of "truth" for the ones that matter inside the narrative, King Hrothgar and his retinue, is that Beowulf survives after such a long time under the water—so long, in fact, that the Danes give him up for dead when the first bright blood appears on the surface of the lake, and depart for home in the "ninth hour." Moreover, Beowulf brings Grendel's head as proof of his feat, and the hilt of a magic sword which he has found among the treasures in the subaquatic cave, and used to slay the monster's mother. In effect, such tangible evidence is brought out of the borderland reality and into the real world of men as a justification of the hero's claims to his rewards, which are promptly given in token of the King's gratitude. For the audience, it is the King's reaction (as much as the actual "proof" Beowulf brings), together with a certain measure of willing credulity—given that epic narratives discuss the heroic origins of the audience's own community. The fantastic is thus justified by means of two narrative devices: on the one hand, the hero operates in the semi-historical past of the intended audience, and on the other, a borderland experience of nature helps integrate the supernatural elements.

In the final part of the story, which takes place fifty years later, we find Beowulf as an old man, settled as King in Gautland. In one last heroic exploit of his twilight years, he seeks out a dragon that threatens his people. The narrative dynamics is similar to the Danish episode of the hero's youth: in order to ensure a successful transition from the real world of "ordinary" wars, courtly matters and the wielding of political power to one in which supernatural places and creatures find their natural place, a journey from the centre of power and into the wilds is undertaken. Eventually, the small company commanded by the King reach

a solitary hall of earth, a vault under ground, nigh to the surges of the deep and the warring waves. All filled within was it with cunning work and golden wire. The monstrous guardian eager and ready in battle ancient beneath the earth kept those golden treasures—no easy bargain that for any among men to win. (Tolkien, Beowulf, 83)

The place described is an old barrow-down near a dramatic sea. The narrative formula of the Danish adventure is thus repeated: a king and his retinue leave behind the safety of the royal hall to set out in search of a threatening monster, which inhabits the wilds in a region not too far away from the hall, but far enough to be rendered credible. The borderland which sets the scene for the intervention of the supernatural shares certain features with the liminal area of the Danish mere: it is wild and solitary, the presence of a violent sea underscores the elemental threats, and the prospect of a descent into an underground realm—underwater in the first episode—infested with even more terrible dangers, renders the arrival all the more poignant. To further strengthen the latter quality of the narrative, there is a speech on behalf of the hero who is about to risk his life, which provides the narrator with the possibility to solemnly emphasize all that is at stake on a personal and collective level, after which the hero leaves the others behind on a solitary quest into the underworld:

> Wearing his grim mail he strode up to the stony cliffs, trusting in the strength of one man alone—such is no craven's feat! [He] saw now at the mound's side a stone-arch standing from whence a stream came hurrying from the hill. The boiling water of that spring was hot with deadly fires; no man could long while endure unscorched that deep place nigh the hoard by reason of the dragon's flame. (Tolkien, *Beowulf* 87)

The scene for the intervention of the fantastic is dominated by the wild qualities of nature, tinged by hints of the supernatural: while in Denmark, Grendel and his mother had contaminated the water of the mere and attracted a host of monstrous companions, here, the dragon has poisoned the natural stream, rendering it burning hot and deadly. The place is emotionally charged by the hero's presence, but also by his words, and the political importance of the event, in which the perpetuation not only of an individual King and his court, but of an entire nation, is at stake (in the latter episode, the attack on the dragon is set against the backdrop of the Swedish attacks on the Geat's realm). A natural location is thus charged with the anticipation of the supernatural, but the passing into a location where the ostensibly supernatural element of the dragon dwells, with tangible and deadly results for mortal men, does not take place until a descent into the underworld has been effected.

There are of course well-known epic precedents of this both in the *Odyssey* and the *Aeneid*; episodes which likewise highlight transitions from realism to a fantastic realm. On a larger scale, in the *Odyssey*, it is not until after Ulysses and his crew have sailed off the map and entered the enchanted archipelago—a world informed by fairy tale and myth—that the magic, the monsters and the marvels begin to appear: a threshold is posited and followed by a transition which allows for the natural to be "supernaturalised" and rendered "credible". Not in vain, Ulysses' adventures in the enchanted archipelago are framed by more conventionally realist episodes, in which the larger political and social reality dominates.

It takes, of course, a different context than our present 21st-century worldview to construe this as potentially "real". In classical antiquity, the concepts of *enarges* and *aletheia*, which can be roughly translated as verisimilitude and truth, respectively, were understood differently from how we relate to these concepts today. What mattered was that what was presented as "real" made sense and remained coherent within the fictional narrative framework. As Ford explains,

> [t]ruth in the archaic period is not the same as historical accuracy. In Homer, the word [alêtheia] is used of accounts by human speakers about matters of which it is difficult to know the facts ... A 'true' speech was one that reported precisely and in detail, with scrupulous attention to what one has said before and the consequences of what one is saying. (50)

On the other hand, the concept of enargês, which would be translated more or less as "intensity" or "force", was used to describe "something or someone appearing convincingly before one's eyes ... The word is also used to describe poetry that puts its incidents clearly before the audience's eyes" (Ford 54). In other words, supernatural elements may abound in an epic narrative without ruining its credibility (alêtheia), as long as the poet makes them conform to the internal coherence of the tale, and express them clearly and convincingly.

This is related to Coleridge's famous conception of the "willing suspension of disbelief" (which Tolkien later called "Secondary Belief"); it is a relative "truth" that hinges more upon the craft of the storyteller to convince the audience that the events make sense inside the story, than upon any notions of empirical verifiability. It is also important to remember that the function of epic narratives went beyond mere entertainment: recitations were solemn and ritualised occasions, usually taking place at court, whereby the event of the telling was invested with a solemnity and a profound cultural significance: it was a speech-act that recreated a world to which the audience had once belonged, and which connected it with the cultural fibres of the community where the recital took place—almost (but not quite), like the occasions in which myths were retold ritually in earlier societies. But epic is not the same as myth (as we have explained earlier, it mixes heroic poetry, myth and fairy-tale motifs with a seriousness of purpose), and epic narratives comprise very large worlds, with great historical depth and geographical width, making them (in one sense) apt predecessors for the realist novel.

As opposed to the realist novel, however, epic verisimilitude depends upon a willingness to take myth seriously. The symbolism of the fantastic is woven into the fabric of the tale with subtle threads, moving from the real to the supernatural in a changing landscape informed by poetic descriptions, overwhelming natural manifestations and an emotionally charged discourse. In *Beowulf,* as in many later British fantastic narratives, the influence of Norse mythology, in which a crude and hostile nature has to be conquered or at least placated, and against whose forces all humans eventually succumb, are evident.

Knights of the court and medieval romance narratives

The Norman conquest of 1066 brought not only a French variety of feudalism to England, but also a different kind of courtly etiquette, which would find its corresponding literary expression in what is now commonly referred to as medieval romance. Stories of King Arthur and the Knights of the Round Table had been part of a pan-European literary heritage for several centuries, but it was Chrétien de Troyes, a French poet of the second half of the twelfth century, who invested the stories and episodes referring to the adventures of the knights of the Round

Table with a distinct romance flavour which made Arthur the first international "superhero" with a distinct Northern European air.

As was the case with the epic narratives, in romance literature contemporary themes are frequently expressed by means of stories set in a remote past, with clearly fantastic tinges. However, as opposed to its epic predecessors, in tales of chivalric romance the fantastic quality of the world takes on a vastly more symbolic character. As Jewers puts it, the setting of this kind of literature is a symbolic backdrop that *eludes* verisimilitude (4). Beer, on the other hand, feels that the reality expressed by medieval romance narratives is "multiple and interwoven," containing "mythic levels of suggestion" (9). Personally I believe the term *suggestion* is key to understand how mythical and fantastic themes are expressed here. The old epic gods are now turned into the Christian *God*, who plays an active part in the configuration of the world, manifesting Himself through nature, or by means of other mysterious signs that only the knight-errant is able to perceive due to his special spiritual sensitivity.

The world of medieval romance is so full of supernatural elements that the landscape in which the knights move becomes a dream-like, elusive and symbolic reality without clear perspectives or measurable distances. As a consequence, it lends itself more readily to subjective interpretations of the world. After all, the spiritual education of the knight is one of the key thematic features of this kind of literature, and instruction is frequently found in a personal interpretation of symbols in nature. The poetic image is the primary poetic tool used to confer a particular meaning to the experience. As Stevens says, it is "there to crystallize the meaning of the scene" (147), which would otherwise be lost in the chaos of interlacing adventures, haphazard encounters and incidents, and wealth of descriptive detail. In this way, the landscape itself seems to emerge from and take shape around the main characters (and not the other way around), and the fantastic elements pop up rather gratuitously, as if at the service of the knights, to provide them with adventures or offer opportunities to exhibit their virtues. In England, it was the anonymously written romances Sir Gawain and the *Green Knight, Pearl* and *Sir Orfeo* (c. 1400), that would provide the most quintessential medieval English fantastic narratives in the romance genre.

In the first of the mentioned works, Sir Gawain is Arthur's most trusted and perfect knight, who takes up a very special challenge posed by a mysterious Green Knight, who suddenly appears in court. The Green Knight says that he is ready to have his head cut off, as long as his executor should be willing to travel to the Green Knight's castle a year later, and subject himself to the same procedure. Sir Gawain promptly cuts off the knight's head—only to witness how the victim picks it up from the floor, reminds Gawain of his promise, and leaves Arthur's court with the head in his hand. No attempt is made here to render this episode credible by any external standards—what is more, it occurs in the middle of the royal court, not in some distant and mysterious place which in *Beowulf* made the scene more malleable and receptive to fantastic elements.

This is partly entertainment to delight and amuse, partly instruction of exemplary moral virtues: since Gawain has to do his duty and be true to his word, he sets out in search of the Green Chapel where he is to receive his due, and it is in this part of the narrative that we find examples of a typically romance use of nature. In the first part of the journey, Gawain travels "through the realm of Logres", arriving at "Northern Wales", with the "isles of Anglesey . . . on his left" (Tolkien, Sir Gawain, 50). These are real places in a real geography, but the reader is not given any particular details of the landscape, and the symbolic qualities remain absent. However, as Gawain finds no trace of the Green Chapel, he is forced to leave the known world behind and enter the wilderness, where

> Many a cliff he climbed o'er in countries unknown
> Far fled from his friends without fellowship he rode
> At every wading or water on the way that he passes
> He found a foe before him, save at few for a wonder
> And so foul were they and fell that fight he must needs
> So many a marvel in the mountains he met in those lands
> That t'would be tedious the tenth part to tell you thereof.
> At whiles with worms he wars, and with wolves also,
> At whiles with wood-trolls that wandered in the crags,
> And with bulls and with bears and boars, too, at times;
> And with ogres that hounded him from the height of the fells (50–51)

The descriptions of Gawain's encounters and struggles with foes as formidable as wood-trolls, wolves, dragons and ogres are dashed off almost casually and formulaically—the narrator even explicitly admits that it would be tedious to tell even a tenth part of all that Gawain had to go through. It is tedious, of course, because these struggles are mere background decoration, stock adventures on the road to the real trial, which truly tests his moral virtues. The wilds in *Sir Gawain*, as in most medieval romance, are so full of monsters and strange beings that it seems almost as if the authors kept a bestiary ready on their writing table, from which they could randomly pull out all manner of fell creatures to spice up the narrative whenever the need should arise. Such monsters are wiped out efficiently, staunchly and dutifully by the knight, but they are not central to the experience. The mystery and the truly fantastic in these narratives are rather located in the human soul, and the sensitivity and moral virtues of the mortal knight are what really matter, not his superhuman strength. Hence, the truly important adventure of Gawain occurs in the mysterious castle he finds in the depths of the woods, where an absent king has left his queen, whose sexual delights and invitations Gawain needs to resist.

The surroundings of this mysterious castle are not ostensibly possessed of any supernatural qualities (though they are vaguely hinted at), but they are described in terms that would famously be labelled "romantic" by later writers and commentators, and the ambience imposed by such descriptions would have an enormous impact on the atmospheres evoked in nineteenth and twentieth-century fantasy narratives. As Gawain delves deeper into the wild lands, he comes

> into a forest that was deep and fearsomely wild,
> with high hills at each hand, and hoar woods beneath
> of huge aged oaks by the hundred together;
> the hazel and the hawthorn were huddled and tangled
> with rough ragged moss around them trailing,
> with many birds bleakly on the bare twigs sitting
> that piteously piped there for pain of the cold.
> . . . a mansion he marked within a moat in the forest,
> on a low mound above a lawn, laced under the branches
> of many a burly bole round about by the ditches:
> the castle most comely that ever a king possessed
> placed amid a pleasaunce with a park all about it,
> within a palisade of pointed pales set closely
> that took its turn round the trees for two miles or more.

> Gawain from the one side gazed on the stronghold
> As it shimmered and shone through the shining oaks (52–53)

The castle and its immediate surroundings are presented as an enclave of civilization in the midst of a wilderness, which provides relief from the dangers of the outside world, together with comfort for both body and soul, as the knight is about to discover. Over the centuries, this archetypal approach to a dwelling in the woods was be filtered by subsequent narrative renderings and echoed in works of children's literature (Grahame's Wild Woods, with Badger's comfortable underground home in its midst, comes to mind), and modern fantasy (such as Tolkien's terrifying Old Forest, balanced by the relief found in Tom Bombadil's snug cottage). The descriptions emphasize the passing from a menacing nature (pictured as "fearsome", "deep", "wild", "high", "hoar", "huge", "tangled", "rough" and "ragged"), which suddenly and almost miraculously gives way to its very opposite: a "comely", well-protected castle that seems to shine with a light of its own, surrounded by an ample "pleasaunce with a park". This is the very image of law and order, an idealized vision of all that aristocracy (the intended audience of this type of narrative) aspired to: it is a godly place, full of spiritual virtues, but also one of physical pleasure, in the midst of a hostile world. Gawain's virtues are tested, both by the queen and the knight, and he narrowly prevails (albeit only after having yielded in some measure to the carnal temptations), learning an important lesson, taught through his example to the audience (desiring both entertainment and moral instruction).

A similar rendering of such a place and atmosphere from the same period, although with a more sinister twist to it, is found in *Sir Orfeo*, a work also commonly attributed to the anonymous author of *Gawain*. In *Sir Orfeo*, legends and myths of Classical Antiquity have been adapted to a British setting and a medieval audience. This was common enough in the period—the most famous example in English literature is Chaucer's adaptation of the story of Troilus and Criseyde (1380s)—but what matters here is not so much the Classical influence as the medievalised fantasy atmosphere, and how nature contributed to it. *Sir Orfeo* is here an English king, whose Queen is taken to fairyland by the King of the fairies and his retinue. Unlike Gawain, who sets out to conquer the wilds and the deadly challenge of the Green Knight, Sir Orfeo is unable to

keep up appearances without his queen, so he renounces his kingship
and goes off into the wild to live a humble life as a ragged wanderer.
Here, however, another fairy-like reality begins to make its presence felt
in the woods:

> There often by him would he see,
> When noon was hot on leaf and tree,
> The king of Faërie with his rout
> Came hunting in the woods about
> With blowing far and crying dim,
> And barking hounds that were with him (179)

Yet another archetypal image of medieval romance—and perhaps even
more importantly, a sound—is here transmitted: the supernatural royal
hunt in the woods with its sounds of the elusive hunting horns of Faery,
heard in the distance. The scene is partly derived from autochthonous
Celtic myth, in which Arawn is a master hunter, magician and Lord of
the Underworld[1], and has since been much repeated in fantastic modes of
literary discourse, most famously by Tennyson ("the horns of Elfland" in
'The Splendour Falls'), Lord Dunsany (*The King of Elfland's Daughter*),
and, of course, by Tolkien, both in the shape of the hunting god Oromë in
The Silmarillion, and the elusive Wood-elves of Mirkwood in *The Hobbit*.

One day, Sir Orfeo recognizes his Queen among the ladies in the
fairy-like retinue, and sets out after them:

> Right into a rock the ladies rode
> And in behind he fearless strode
> He went into that rocky hill
> A good three miles or more, until
> He came into a country fair
> As bright as sun in summer air.
> Level and smooth it was and green,
> And hill nor valley there was seen.
> A castle he saw amid the land
> Princely and proud and lofty stand;
> The outer wall around it laid
> Of shining crystal clear was made. (181)

---

1 Arawn famously appears in the First and Fourth Branches of the Welsh *Mabinogion*.

The description mixes the magic fairy-tale castle made of crystal with the romance quest of the knight, and both combine with the ancient myth of Sir Orfeo as his namesake discovers that he has entered the realm of the dead. Among other specters in this strange world, Sir Orfeo discovers the dead body of his wife, the Queen, under a tree in an orchard. He offers his services as minstrel to the King of Faërie, who is so pleased with the music that he in turn asks Sir Orfeo to pick anything he likes in the castle as a reward. Orfeo, of course, chooses his queen, and the King reluctantly grants his gift (but only after Sir Orfeo has appealed to the chivalric code of honour which involves being true to one's word).

In this tale, nature again acts like a canvas for fantastic incidents and elements, but as opposed to *Sir Gawain*, their presence is less frivolous. As in *Beowulf*, there is a transition into a borderland (the wilds in which the depressed Sir Orfeo takes refuge) which paves the way for the crossing of a more ostensible threshold—the rock, and the tunnel, that leads under it and into the Otherworld of the dead.

Sublime nature in Gothic narratives[2]

After an impasse of several centuries, during which the enormous impact of Renaissance humanism and post-Renaissance Enlightenment practically did away with fantastic narratives in mainstream literature, the Romance impulse returned without the satirical purposes of a Rabelais or a Swift. In terms of spatial representation, one of the focal points of this new fascination with pre-Enlightenment and medieval sensibilities were the ruins of monasteries, scattered across the English countryside, that had been destroyed during the Reformation. Such broken remains turned into a suitable symbolic space for meditations on a national past, recent as well as more ancient, reaching back as far as the decline and fall of the Roman Empire. The influential statesman, philosopher and

---

2   Parts of this section have been adapted from Simonson's introduction to *Gothic Horror: The Castle of Otranto and The Monk* (Montero 2016).

writer Edmund Burke (1729–1797) wrote about the sublimity and power of Stonehenge in his influential essay *Philosophical Enquiry into the Origin of the Beautiful and the Sublime* (1756), emphasizing the feelings of awe inspired by such monuments and scenes. In Botting's words,

> The vastness that had been glimpsed in the natural sublime became the mirror of the immensity of the human mind. Elevating and expanding mental powers to an almost divine extent signified the displacement of religious authority and mystery by the sublimity of nature and the human imagination. (38)

The new emphasis on secular imagination, as opposed to secular *reason*, would have far-reaching consequences. Up until the 1760's, post-Elizabethan English literature had not really been able to liberate imagination from religion: Milton is one case in point, as is the more recent "Graveyard" school of poetry, which focused on gloomy aspects of reality that had been neglected by contemporary mainstream culture. Poems such as Robert Blair's *The Grave* (1743) and Edward Young's *Night Thoughts* (1744–45) feature lugubrious scenes with an emphasis on night, death, tombs and ghosts, but they were less a celebration of the irrational or the secular imagination than cautionary tales intended for impious readers who were meant to reflect upon dark sins and impending doom.

The allure of the native past, mixed with awe-inspiring natural sceneries and a secular imagination, were as natural a part of eighteenth-century English culture as the officially approved standards of verisimilitude in literature, or the politically sanctioned stress on reason as the true vehicle of progress. In literature, this antiquarianism prompted several literary re-imaginations of the medieval past. James Macpherson's alleged "translations" of Ossian (1760–1765) are perhaps the most paradigmatic example of the new urge to capture the spirit of the Middle Ages by conjuring up a modern rendering based on ancient medieval sources. However, the most influential literary work of the period was Horace Walpole's *The Castle of Otranto* (1764), which likewise claimed to be a translation of a medieval manuscript and signaled the emergence of the so-called gothic novel, "a 'blend' of the 'imagination and improbability' found in ancient romance, and the accurate imitation of nature that is the hallmark of the modern novel" (Clery xii).

Nightmares and the unconscious had previously been firmly anchored in the world of superstitions and irrational fears, contrary to the ideals of the enlightened eighteenth century, but here Walpole, with unabashed zest, introduced a whole range of sinister and ostensibly supernatural elements in his narrative without any clear didactic message concerning their dangers. The explosive combination of supernatural intervention and underground crypts and ruins of a distant past, set in a distant land, caused a sensation that exposed the inherent contradictions of an age obsessed with reason. In Botting's view, "gothic fancy and invention were able to construct other worlds that dislocated barriers between fact and fiction, history and contemporaneity, reality and fantasy" (49).

A new aesthetic sensibility, informed by the antiquarian interest of the period, tinged the displacement in space and time. One of the consequences of this was a re-assessment of Spenser, whose epic romance *The Faerie Queene* had been regarded with certain suspicion by the enlightened English society. However, in *Observations* on the Fairy Queen of Spenser (1754), Warton changed this view: "It was [Spenser's] business to engage the fancy, and to interest the attention by bold and striking images ... The various and the marvellous were the chief sources of delight" (qtd. in Williamson 55). Such attitudes are emblematic of the new sensibility, and medieval romance became an obvious imaginative source of inspiration, filtered through the increasingly popular imagery associated with sublime manifestations of nature.

Another common feature of the Gothic novel is its emphasis on dark and encroaching spaces. Characters frequently find themselves locked up in the ever-present underground vaults, burial chambers and graves, or otherwise isolated from the protective sphere of the civilized world in dense forests or among bleak mountains. There is of course a strong presence of the sublime in the craggy peaks, the ruins of abbeys and the wild natural sceneries, but the main emotional effect of the setting is not one of awe in the mixed sense of fear and admiration, but rather one of oppression. The darkness, isolation and general vulnerability of the characters underscore the essential fragility of the human condition.

Here is Isabella, one of the main characters of *The Castle of Otranto*, exploring the subterranean regions of the castle alluded to in the title:

> She felt for the door, and having found it, entered trembling into the vault from
> whence she had heard the sigh and steps. It gave her a kind of momentary joy to
> perceive an imperfect ray of clouded moonshine gleam from the roof of the vault,
> which seemed to be fallen in, and from whence hung a fragment of earth or build-
> ing she could not distinguish which, that appeared to have been crushed inwards.
> She advanced eager towards this chasm, when she discerned a human form stand-
> ing close against the wall. (Walpole 39)

The Gothic novel depends to a great extent on the creation of an oppres-
sive and threatening atmosphere to set the scene for violent emotions and
fear, which is the intended response of the reader. Nature interacts with
the ruins of man-made structures, now haunted by ghosts, which recalls
a more primitive state of civilization, full of superstitions and horror.
Part of the excitement stems from the innocence of the young protagonists, in turn informed by an aesthetic sensibility that implores them to
explore such recesses of the past (and of their own minds):

> Theodor at length determined to repair to the forest that Matilda had pointed out
> to him. Arriving there, he sought the gloomiest shades, as best suited to the pleas-
> ing melancholy that reigned in his mind. In this mood he roved insensibly to the
> caves which had formerly served as a retreat to hermits, and were now reported
> around the country to be haunted by evil spirits. (Walpole 66)

For the remaining years of the eighteenth century, many writers experimented with the possibilities of the new genre, combining it with the
trappings of the realist novel and adding further layers of significance
and subtleties to the original approach. In Walpole's *Otranto*, the settings had been rather schematically described, but Clara Reeve (*The Old
English Baron*) and Ann Radcliffe (*The Mysteries of Udolpho, The Ital-
ian*)—together with many other less known writers—invested them with
intricately wrought details, reflective of the appearance of the romanti-
cally sublime landscapes that had begun to appear in poetry, narrative
fiction and landscape painting. In this process, whether due to personal
taste or as a concession to the standards of verisimilitude they felt were
required by the form of the novel, more often than not the supernatural
elements were rationalized and explained away.

In *The Monk* (1796), on the other hand, Matthew Gregory Lewis
ostensibly poked fun at such concessions, while making use of the Rad-
cliffean Gothic sensibility in his descriptions of nature:

I concealed the carriage in a spacious cavern of the hill, on whose brow the castle was situated: this cavern was of considerable depth, and among the peasants was known by the name of Lindeberg Hole. The night was calm and beautiful: the moonbeams fell upon the ancient towers of the castle, and shed upon their summits a silver light. All was still around me: nothing was to be heard except the night breeze sighing among the leaves, the distant barking of village dogs, or the owl who had established herself in a nook of the deserted eastern turret. I heard her melancholy shriek, and looked upwards. She sat upon the ride of a window, which I recognized to be that of the haunted room. (Lewis 182)

In this way, the gothic novel re-introduces romance on the European literary scene, but this time through the medium of the novel, the influence of which can be seen in the descriptions of places and situations. The geography is usually quite exact, and even if the coincidences on which the plot often rests are totally improbable, at least they conform to the internal coherence of the story, making the genre lean closer to the realist novel than to traditional romance narratives. This use of a physical space which is described more or less realistically as the setting for supernatural and mysterious events, had a notable influence on the nineteenth-century writers of prose romances and fantastic novels that pulled the novel standards even further towards the imaginative realm. The gothic novels of the eighteenth century would also be a source of inspiration for the Romantic literary movement, above all due to the implications of the subconscious powers that inform them, but also because of their particular vision of the Middle Ages.

Nature in 19th-century prose romances

The supernatural acquires many hues in the Romantic and Victorian periods. While the Romantic sensibility was pervasive throughout the nineteenth century, and could be appreciated in works by writers as varied as Mary Shelley, Stevenson, Haggard, Stoker and Wells, there were also the 'original' fairy tales, and, towards the end of the century, the pseudo-medieval prose romances of William Morris.

At the beginning of the century, traditional fairy tales were an important source of inspiration for many writers, especially for the German Romantics, such as Novalis, E.T.A. Hoffmann, Ludwig Tieck, Friedrich de la Motte Foqué and others, who—informed by philosophers like Fichte, Herder and Schiller—saw in them clear manifestations of mankind's essential desires and concerns, but also the "authentic" expression of cultural roots. English Romantic poets and artists were inspired by these folk tales, but the English versions of the genre would adopt a slightly different form, and the interest in folk tales did not cease with the progressive decadence of Romantic values; instead, it was prolongated into the Victorian era, and generated a favourable intellectual climate for the creation of original English fairy tales.

Manlove (11–12) divides this literature into two main fields: comic and imaginative fantasy. In his view, the first category corresponds to works of authors like Thackeray or Nesbit, aiming merely at entertaining their readers. In the second category we would find the narratives of writers such as MacDonald, Kingsley and Morris, who attempted to convey a totalizing vision of a fantastic world that appears as real as our own.

George MacDonald and William Morris were two of the most successful imaginative writers of the nineteenth century. Morris began publishing fantastic tales in 1856 (*The Hollow Land*), while MacDonald's novel *Phantastes*, the story of a man whose chamber is turned into a great forest that swallows him, appeared in 1858. In spite of the fact that the two writers had very different personalities and interests—MacDonald was a theologian, whereas Morris was a convinced socialist—they are commonly regarded as the main forerunners of the genre known today as fantasy literature, together with Sara Coleridge's *Phantasmion*, which Williamson considers to be the first real sustained prose narrative of modern fantasy (87).

Sara Coleridge, MacDonald and Morris are the first writers to design, describe and develop invented worlds with an internal coherence as a complete spatial framework for their stories. They had several reasons to do so. Landow (132) suggests that Morris's novels *The Well at the World's End* and *The Water of the Wondrous Isles* are the result of a creation of worlds in which the writer could dramatize the spiritual problems of contemporary society with greater poignancy. Zanger, for his part, believes that both Morris and MacDonald "turned to fantasy as an alternative to the utilitarian world of hard fact and Victorian bourgeois commodity culture [proposing] an ordered society instead of the social disorders created by the Industrial Revolution" (179).

Such expressions are prone to display idealized landscapes without the sinister dimension of the Gothic novel. In MacDonald's *Phantastes*, Anodos, the protagonist, is transported through a kind of dream vision to a fantastic world, marked by a medievalised, lush nature in stark contrast to the industrial reality of contemporary England. Waking up in his own room one morning, he finds himself on the borders of Fairy Land, where the furniture and the room itself are merging with this alternative reality:

> My dressing-table was an old-fashioned piece of furniture of black oak, with drawers all down the front. These were elaborately carved in foliage, of which ivy formed the chief part. The nearer end of this table remained just as it had been, but on the further end a singular change had commenced. I happened to fix my eye on a little cluster of ivy-leaves. The first of these was evidently the work of the carver; the next looked curious; the third was unmistakably ivy, and just beyond it a tendril of clematis had twined itself about the gilt handle of one of the drawers ... springing from the bed, my feet alighted upon a cool green sward [and] I found myself completing my toilet under the boughs of a great tree, whose top waved in the golden stream of the sunrise with many interchanging lights, and with shadows of leaf and branch gliding over leaf and branch, as the cool morning wind swung it to and fro, like a sinking sea-wave. (MacDonald 9–10)

The emphasis falls on the experience of leaving the old, disenchanted world behind and being invigorated by a refreshing nature, based on a romanticized conception of medieval England, which provides a spiritual nourishment for the Victorian protagonist that was lacking, it is implied, in the contemporary industrial world.

Fuelled, among other things, by the Pre-raphaelite rediscovery of the Middle Ages, by new editions of mythological tales directly or indirectly related to the cultural heritage of the British Isles—George Dasent's translation of the *Prose Edda* in 1842 and Lady Charlotte Guest's translation of *The Mabinogion*, published between 1838–1849, were the two most influential works in this context—; by Ruskin's prolific and widely disseminated insistence on the communal value of art, and by Tennyson's Arthurian romance *The Idylls of the King* (1859–1885), the polifacetic William Morris indirectly criticized the materialistic aspects of Victorian society and its blind faith in progress in his utopian novels, *A Dream of John Ball* (1888) and *News From Nowhere* (1890). However, it was with *The House of the Wolfings* (1888) and *The Roots of the Mountains* (1889) that he used pseudo-medieval mythical structures to greatest effect in his attempt to propose alternative social modes of life. Of *The House of the Wolfings*, Mathews highlights the communal values and the symbolic representation of a female identity through Mother Earth and the Sun, while arguing that *The Roots of the Mountains* establishes the use of "imagined landscape as an important symbolic and creative element of fantasy that places even greater importance on geography and on elemental symbols—water, wood, mountain, plain" (43). This combination, leaning towards a good measure of realism, comes through in descriptive prose such as the following:

> The upper end of the valley, where it first began to open out from the pass, was rugged and broken by rocks and ridges of water-born stones, but presently it smoothed itself into mere grassy swelling and knolls, and at last into a fair and fertile plain swelling up into a green wave, as it were, against the rock-wall that encompassed it on all sides save where the river came gushing out of the strait pass at the east end, and where at the west end it poured itself out of the Dale toward the lowlands and the plain of the great river.

> Now the valley was some ten miles of our measure from that place of the rocks and the stone ridges, to where the faces of the hills drew somewhat anigh to the river again at the west, and then fell back along the edge of the great plain... (Morris, *More to William Morris*, 99)

The passage shows an almost obsessive wish to provide the imagined world with accuracy and verisimilitude, emphasizing the natural features of the setting. *The House of the Wolfings* and *The Roots of the Mountains*, together with *The Story of the Glittering Plain or the Land of Living Men*, (1891) and *The Wood Beyond the World* (1894), pointed towards Morris's most accomplished work, *The Well at the World's End* (1896), in which the author manages to crystallize his vision and purpose in one single, if extensive, narrative. Here, Morris uses a great variety of popular legends, fairy tales, and heroic myths, placing the combination of these elements in an invented, pseudo-medieval world and using heroic action as the main thread of the story. In terms of the representation of nature, it is clearly informed by the Arts and Crafts-standards that

Morris himself was so instrumental in establishing, according to which nature acts as a guiding principle for human art.

When Ralph and Ursula at long last reach the Well at the World's End that lends its name to the novel, the place is pictured as a natural element enhanced by human intervention, and imbued with a supernatural life force:

> Just below the place where they stood, right up against the cliff, was builded by man's hands of huge stones a garth or pound, the wall whereof was some seven feet high ... and the said pound was filled with the waters of a spring that came forth from the face of the cliff ... the water of the Well came gushing forth from a hollow therein in a great swelling as clear as glass; and the sun glistened in it and made a foam-bow about its edges. (Morris, *The Well at the World's End*, Vol II, Book III, 92)

While the water is imbued with divine powers, the magical quality of the experience is enhanced both by natural elements and by man's art, in a typically Pre-raphaelite or Arts and Crafts-conception of the fantastic. This type of setting, in which the invented world itself is both realistically portrayed and infused with magic through the combination of natural features and man-made improvements, would later, in the twentieth century, be used by many other writers, giving rise to a subgenre of fantastic literature called "high fantasy", or "heroic fantasy" and which included works by writers such as Dunsany, Eddison, Tolkien, Moorcock and Le Guin.

II Edwardian Reconfigurations of the Poetics of Nature and Fantasy

The Victorian *fin de siècle* was crucial as a catalyst for the complex marriage between the celebration of the natural world and literary versions of fairy stories that would shape so much of the fantasy literature written in the twentieth century. In Britain, the emphasis falls on an Englishness with roots that lie in the country, not the city, and a desire to rekindle wonder and explore Otherness in a familiar setting just around the corner—which, after a deeper scrutiny, turns out to be awe-inspiring and hold the essential and primal stuff of which myths are made.

The late Victorian and the Edwardian periods were in many ways a confusing and contradictory moment in history, as so many are. The Edwardian times used to be seen as a period of perpetual golden summers and garden parties, in which Siegfried Sassoon would spend leisurely hours playing golf or, in moments of greater zest, hunt foxes, while the Stephen sisters, later known as Virginia Woolf and Vanessa Bell, would receive brilliant intellectuals in their home in Bloomsbury, and Kenneth Grahame would retire from his public office as the Secretary of the Bank of England to his Oxfordshire cottage, finally enjoying the *adult* version of countryside bliss he had written so much about in his books for children.

However, from the 1960's on, this picture of the times was contested, notably by historians like Samuel Hynes, who in his influential 1968 study *The Edwardian Turn of Mind* debunked such notions, stressing the inherent tensions of the age, related to the "conflict between old and new ideas" (7) on all levels of society. While the conservatives still had a strong foothold, the proponents of the new were increasingly active. In Hynes' words, "This sense of the time as one of liberation from the Victorian past was very strong among advanced groups, and it must be understood if one is to properly understand the Edwardian period" (9). This new conception of the Edwardian period would cause later writers and historians to claim that, contrary to the myth, modernity was not brought to England by the Great War—it had already taken place. As Roy Hattersley confidently asserts in *The Edwardians* (2004): "Modern Britain was born in the opening years of the twentieth century. It is the legacy of the Edwardians" (481). Hattersley further holds that the age saw "a political and social revolution, accompanied and sustained by an explosion of intellectual and artistic energy [which] swept England into the modern world" (1). Others, however, have taken a more tempered view of things. Modris Eksteins, for example, felt that both the Victorian and the Edwardian periods "were ages seeking certitude" (128). Eksteins continues: "In values and judgements on issues of decency, the family, social and political order, and religion, the Edwardians were extensions of the Victorians. That there was a greater threat of change and a stronger sense of challenge afoot in the later era, that was the difference" (130).

Such threats stemmed in part from the Anglo-German Naval Arms Race and the disastrous Boer wars of the 1890's, both of which undoubtedly served to question Britain's role as the world's leading nation and colonial power. In Victorian times, Britain's global power, based on capitalist practices, had been ingeniously justified through references to the virtues of liberalism and utilitarianism by proponents such as John Stuart Mill. However, new players in the political field were emerging, among others the socialist Fabian Society, which in the early years of the century helped the Labour Party bring about reforms that would shake the foundations of the traditional English society.

In this revised picture of the times, cultural historians often highlight the conflict between tradition and modernity which operated upon the Edwardian mind in all fields of art and politics. Such anxieties could take different expressions. In literature, the imagist and Vorticist experimentation of Ezra Pound and others found a contrast in the traditional Georgian poetry of Rupert Brooke and Edward Thomas, while E.M. Forster's and Joseph Conrad's realist accounts of the age coexisted with Lord Dunsany's fantasy tales set in secondary worlds, and the presence of fairies in children's literature and drama—most spectacularly in J.M. Barries' enormously successful *Peter Pan* (first staged in 1904)—was ubiquitous.[3] Not in vain, J.R.R. Tolkien, the most influential writer of

---

3   The presence of fairies in theatrical plays enjoyed a long-standing and prestigious tradition in Britain thanks to Shakespeare, and was widely popularized also in art.

fantasy in the twentieth century, found his own voice through his readings and his upbringing in late Victorian and Edwardian England. Before we discuss the impact of Tolkien, however, we will take a brief look at how nature was portrayed in the works of literary fantasy written in the Edwardian period.

English landscapes and fantasy in Edwardian literature[4]

In the Edwardian period, the increasingly sharp lines of division between tradition and modernity, countryside and urban life, imagination and reason, myth and realism, the autochthonous and the foreign (Simonson 2020), informed a type of literature that involved a peculiar marriage of nature writing and fantasy. The countryside, for writers combining both strands, was more than just a recreational space—it turned into a natural catalyst of the mentioned tensions, in which the atmosphere of nostalgia for a vanishing countryside, this repository of disappearing spiritual and cultural values, took the shape of mythical and fantastic narratives. In this way, a very modern fantastic discourse, that was simultaneously reaching back to the past, was integrated into the very fabric of the early twentieth-century English landscape by literary explorers, who wished to probe the depths of nature in order to unearth vestiges of older history and myth that might provide some measure of solace in the face of contemporary anxieties.

This particular strain of nature writing and fantasy was Romantic in origin (Lobdell 10) and more or less detached from the period's industrial reality, which was reflected obliquely, or by way of negative example (if at all). The most important Victorian precedent for this peculiar

---

According to Iain Zaczek, "in the late eighteenth century, when the authorities were trying to promote a national school of British art, the depiction of Shakespearean subjects was actively encouraged" (12), and fairies were foremost among the preferred subjects.

4 Parts of the analysis of Edwardian fantasy, and how it was informed by transcendence and natural explorations, have been adapted from Simonson (2020).

combination was William Morris, often considered the father of modern fantasy, who combined the English natural settings and medievalism in his highly popular prose romances of the 1890's, as we have seen. However, Morris, whose literary expressions were filtered by Pre-Raphaelite versions of Romanticism, Arts and Crafts-principles and Socialist convictions, was only one of the influences. Another important predecessor was Richard Jefferies, who combined his writing about nature with fantasy in his 1881 novel *Wood Magic*. In Jefferies' postapocalyptic tale *After London*, written four years later, nature has reclaimed the land and the remaining humans revert to a medieval lifestyle.

Another related current in literature was the Victorian adventure story, largely inherited from Rider Haggard's novels about British explorers and adventurers in remote and exotic corners of the Empire—*King Solomon's Mines* (1882) and *She* (1887), among others—, was perpetuated in the Edwardian period by writers such as Algernon Blackwood (*The Centaur*, 1910) and Conan Doyle (*The Lost World*, 1912). In spite of their exoticism, both literary strands had an ideological impact on the development of the autochthonous crossbreed between nature and fantasy of the period. For one thing, the stories are indebted to older quest narratives and imbued with a sense of wonder at natural marvels. As Lobdell says in his discussion of characterisation in this type of stories, it is largely about "the character of nature"; it is "a story of Englishmen abroad in the wide and mysterious world ... looking for ... the wide world itself", and doing so, "they sense a mysterious character indwelling in the world itself ... the idea of the past mysteriously alive in the present" (15–17).

The Edwardian literary crossbreed of nature-writing and fantasy would normally be written by members of the middle class, who, largely thanks to Morris, would be influenced by medieval traditions and leaning towards older values of the aristocracy in their re-assessment of the native English landscape. They filtered the previous expressions of Morris and Jefferies and projected the genre into the future, clearing the way for such diverse writers as J.R.R. Tolkien and H.P. Lovecraft, both of whom were born in the early 1890's and grew up while the late Victorian and Edwardian fantasy literature flourished. The fact that a reassessment of the English countryside can be found both in children's literature and in a new vein of horror stories by Machen and Blackwood, written for adults and derived from Stevenson, Wilde, and the so-called decadent writers of the 1890's, testifies to the flexibility of the imaginative possibilities offered by such a reassessment of the English countryside in these years.

Children's literature, nature and fantasy

The idealization of the country, seasoned with a dash of fantasy and involving an exploration of past traditions with nature as a catalyst, was part and parcel of several of the most popular children's tales of the period. Kenneth Grahame's *The Wind in the Willows,* Edith Nesbit's many works and Beatrix Potter's fables were all ostensibly set in rural milieus where the protagonists could explore alternative realities far from the supervision of adults and constrictive urban environments. In parallel, nature writing had developed into a genre of its own in this period, notably through the work of writers like Richard Jefferies, W.H. Hudson and Edward Thomas. However, even this genre could be permeated by more fantastic narrative modes. As Bunce says, the countryside in children's literature provides the reader with "a familiar yet at the same time imaginary world" (64), and this is seen in the work of both Grahame and Potter, where animals are representatives of country people, with different attitudes to society and culture, which sometimes come into contact with a deeper, supernatural presence that inhabits the land they believed to be familiar, but which turns out to be a thoroughly strange place. In Grahame's *The Wind in the Willows*, Rat and Mole set out in a small boat on the river Thames before dawn, in search of a lost Otter-child. As they row on, and dawn slowly breaks, they behold a vision:

A wide half-circle of foam and glinting lights and shining shoulders of green water, the great weir closed the backwater from bank to bank, troubled all the quiet surface with twirling eddies and floating foam-streaks, and deadened all other sounds with its solemn and soothing rumble. In midmost of the stream, embraced in the weir's shimmering arm-spread, a small island lay anchored, fringed close with willows and silver birch and alder. Reserved, shy, but full of significance, it hid whatever it might hold behind a veil, keeping it till the hour should come, and, with the hour, those who were called and chosen. (Grahame, *The Wind in the Willows*, 122)

As it turns out, it is Pan who is sitting on the island, playing his flute. As soon as the sun rises, however, the vision is broken, and the two companions are back in the real world again. Bunce feels that the fact that this type of literature is predominantly British "has much to do with the general national sentimentality towards the countryside" (66), but this specifically British type of sentimentality gives rise to stories aimed at evoking a sense of wonder. Clayton Hamilton sums up his 1910 interview with Grahame in the following way:

> The most priceless possession of the human race is the wonder of the world. Yet, latterly, the utmost endeavours of mankind have been directed towards the dissipation of that wonder ... Nobody, any longer, may hope to entertain an angel unawares, or to meet Sir Launcelot in shining armour on a moonlit road. In my tales about children, I have tried to show that their simple acceptance of the mood of wonderment, their readiness to welcome a perfect miracle at any hour of the day or night, is a thing more precious than any of the laboured acquisitions of the adult mankind. (qtd. in Prince 254–255)

Grahame's biographer Alison Prince adds: "All his writing makes it clear that God, to [Grahame], was self-evidently present in the continuum which is inherent in nature" (301). Other works in the same tradition also aim at evoking this almost Wordsworthian sense of wonder, in which nature acts as a mediator and facilitator of an enhanced understanding of our own place in history and nature. It is in the half-wild, half-domesticated countryside of Sussex that the children in Rudyard Kipling's *Puck of Pook's Hill* (1906) enact a rendering of *A Midsummer Night's Dream* on Midsummer Eve, and bring forth the Puck character of ancient folklore and Shakespeare's play:

> A cuckoo sat on a gate-post singing his broken June-tune, 'cucko cuk', while a busy kingfisher crossed from the mill-stream to the brook which ran on the other side of the meadow. Everything else was a sort of thick, sleepy stillness smelling of meadow-sweet and dry grass ... This was when they heard a whistle among the alders on the bank, and they jumped ... they saw a small, brown, broad-shouldered, pointy-eared person with a snub nose, slanting blue eyes, and a grin that ran right across his freckled face ... He pointed to the bare, fern-covered slope of Pook's Hill that runs up from the far side of the mill-stream to a dark wood. Beyond that wood the ground rises and rises for five hundred feet, till at last

you climb out on the bare top of Beacon Hill, to look over the Pevensey Levels and the Channel and half of the naked South Downs.

"By Oak, and Ash, and Thorn!" he cried, still laughing. "If this had happened a few hundred years ago, you'd have had all the People of the Hills out like bees in June!" (Kipling 5–8)

Puck then proceeds to show the children the marvels of the legendary, mythical and semi-historical English past, introducing them to a number of characters from different periods.

This type of flirtation with the world of fairies had solid precedents in British nineteenth-century culture, largely thanks to Shakespeare. As Jessica Burke explains, fairies in Elizabethan times "involved the so-called unexplainable things in life ... They ranged in purpose from helpful spirits who tinkered about the house or farm, to kidnapping specters reminiscent of the revenant" (28–29). In Shakespeare's rendering of fairies, they are no longer a thing to be feared, having instead been turned into the frivolous and rather silly beings of diminutive stature that we find in plays such as *A Midsummer Night's Dream* (1595–6) and *The Tempest* (1610–11). In Victorian times, the Shakespearean fairies were popularized by the numerous stage productions of his plays and the accompanying vogue for fairy-painting, which arose as pictorial renderings of scenes from *A Midsummer Night's Dream* and reached its peak in the period between 1840 and 1870, mainly through the works of Richard Dadd, John Anster Fitzgerald and Joseph Noël Paton (Burke 31). Particularly influential were the stage productions of Elizabeth Vestries, whose "fairies were no longer stately Muses, or sylphs: instead, they donned insect-like wings and crowns of flowers and were remade in the Victorian image" (Burke 33). In Burke's words, fairies became "outlets through which many divergent facets of the Victorian psyche were brought together[, f]rom exploration into spiritualism and the occult, to an expression of undaunted sexuality" (32). Later in the century, however, a certain strand of fairy painting would move away from the sweet and whimsical representations of the earlier Victorian period to more frightening images, as in the works of Edmund Dulac and John Anster Fitzgerald, notably in the latter's famous "The Stuff That Dreams Are Made Of" (Burke 32).

Such was the culturally imbued heritage of fairies that reached the Edwardian times, which produced its own versions of fairies in literature and art. The more sinister versions were to some extent reinforced by the Pan-cult, related to the Aesthetic movement of the 1890's (Prince 90–94), which merged with the Victorian idea of fairies and found its way into children's fantasy stories, such as the previously mentioned works by Kipling and Grahame, and, of course, J.M. Barrie's *Peter Pan* (1910).

In these works (with the notable exception of *Peter Pan*) the appearance of fairies, fairy-like beings and the fantastic are mediated by natural environments—be they a secluded valley in the Sussex countryside, or an isolated stretch of riverbed in the Thames Valley. They emerge in these environments by means of a heightened perception of the natural world, enhanced by the observer's imagination and some half-forgotten knowledge of the mythic and legendary heritage of the local and/or regional (sometimes national) cultural and natural milieu.

Nature, transcendence and fantasy

The idea of nature acting as a wonder-inciting gateway between the known world and some transcendental region was also expressed in another type of literature, in which the liminal space between the Edwardian everyday reality and the potentially wonder-inspiring world of nature is not merely perceived, but more consciously *explored*, and in these works nature is sometimes rendered dangerous and frightening. Nature is here construed not only as an old home to which we no longer belong completely, but also one which can destroy us. This obviously echoes the Romantic notions of the sublime, and this strain of neo-Romanticism, coupled with the inherited vogue for fairies and the notions of the country as a true repository of myth and national identity, informs much of the treatment of nature in the literature of the period. Even realist writers were affected by it, and novelists like E.M Forster assigned an almost mystical quality to their own, as well as their main characters', experiences of nature and the country (Parker 231).

One of the most accomplished writers of this type of literature is Edward Thomas, who is today perhaps best known for his poetry, but for a period spanning roughly 20 years he also wrote many country books[5], most of them travelogues set in Southern England and Wales. Thomas was born in London but sustained a life-long aversion to city life, as attested by his biographers (Hollis, Helen Thomas), and from an early age he made use of any opportunity he could to escape from the city for long walks in the countryside, especially the counties surrounding London.

Thomas would himself refer to "that country which is dominated by the Downs or by the English Channel, or by both" as "The South Country" (*South Country* 1). For Thomas, who was an incredibly astute observer of the natural world, the region was an imaginatively alluring space, suggestive of old, native and even mythical traditions that were mediated by the natural scenery, and his attempts to capture this half-imaginary, half-real realm in words frequently turn into a quest to unveil cultural strata buried in the landscape. At times, these explorations take on the shape of fantasy narratives in which Thomas unearths and extracts supernatural elements, which he then examines in order to assess their role in the present Edwardian reality. With *The South Country* he set out to write another country book, but in this work the lyrical descriptions of the natural marvels and folk roots often move beyond the ordinary world of perception, and show Thomas trying to find a language to express his fluttering glimpses of the timeless realm hidden beyond ordinary appearances.[6]

In one passage, Thomas reflects on how the smells of nature after rain set off his imagination and bring him a strange joy: "Newly dressed in the crystal of the rain the landscape recalls ... the joys of life that come through the nostrils from the dark, not understood world which

---

5   *Beautiful Wales* (1905), *The Heart of England* (1906), *The South Country* (1909), *The Icknield Way* (1911) and *In Pursuit of Spring* (1913) are the best-known titles.

6   Longley considers that Emerson and Thoreau were "formative writers" for Thomas and hints at their being partly responsible for his "residual mystical inclinations" ('Introduction', *Collected Poems*, 14). Thomas's mystical vision of nature has also been attributed to the influence of Thomas Traherne, an explicit acknowledgment of which is featured in the section "June-Hampshire-The Golden Age-Traherne" of *The South Country* (93–112).

is unbolted for us by the delicate and savage fragrances of leaf and flower. . ." (*South Country* 43). However, the promise of remaining in the world of mystery and vision vanishes with the changing of the light, as the next paragraph shows:

> But at morning twilight I see the moon low in the west like a broken and dinted shield of silver hanging long forgotten outside the tent of a great knight in the wood, and inside are the knight's bones clean and white about his rusted sword[,] and I am ill-content. (*South Country* 43)

History and myth are no longer alive in the present, Thomas implies, because the moment of heightened perception which opened the gates of the "dark, not understood world", depends on a state of mind which is contingent both on the whims of nature and on our own mortal limitations.[7]

In other works, notably in his short stories,[8] Thomas would provide a more sustained expression of his desire to transcend the everyday and enjoy the deeper, supernatural dimension of the English landscape. In "The Queen of the Waste Lands," the concluding tale of the collection *Rest and Unrest* (1910), the narrator is contemplating the English countryside from some vantage point and his inner eye perceives a queenlike figure, who embodies the spirit of the country, with whom he engages in conversation which is worth quoting at some length:

> "Queen of the Waste Lands," said I, "where is your realm? How may it be reached and. . ."
>
> "It is everywhere. You are in the midst of it. This is but one of its provinces. [. . .] The capital of my realm is now here and now there among these islands. It is in your heart this day. Many times it has been in a poet's heart, but there is no heart where it has not been, either in sleep or in solitude, for a little while."
>
> Very sweet was her voice, and as the plover's voice utters the nature of the marsh so hers uttered that of the Waste Lands, of the islands, their graves and

---

7   This obviously recalls some famous Romantic musings on the same subject, such as Keats's *Ode to a Nightingale*, with which Thomas, the critic of poetry, was well acquainted.

8   The ambiguous titles of his two collections of short prose, *Rest and Unrest* (1910) and *Light and Twilight* (1911) are evocative of the general mood both of Thomas and the Edwardian times he lived in.

desolate walls, and of the seas. I loved her, and thinking that she also might love me, I spoke again, saying: "Since you have made your palace, Queen, in this empty heart, make me, I beseech you, one of your company that I may serve you and dwell in your realm for ever and be, under you, one of the lords of the Waste Lands."

"You ask," she said, pitifully, "what is impossible, as others have done before you, and will again. For I dwell alone and have no company among the living. Yet a little while and you shall have your will, though you cannot know it when the day comes. Farewell."

The word sundered me from her and from her realm, and left me discontented with the meadow and its green grass and golden flowers, and the white sheep under the wood, with May and its fulness, with life itself that had the Waste Lands among its many kingdoms. (189–191)

Thomas's inherently melancholy disposition prevented him from being permanently enriched by such fleeting glimpses of timeless nature—in part, probably, because he was stifled by his everyday obligations and hackwork as a literary critic. In this, too, he reflects the contradictory and often frustrated spirit of the Edwardian age.

It was also in the Edwardian period that Algernon Blackwood, who was born in Kent in 1869, came into his own as a writer of imaginative "weird" fiction, ranging from fairy tales and drama (*A Prisoner in Fairy Land,* 1913) to tales of horror ("The Wendigo", 1910), ghost stories (*The Empty House and Other Ghost Stories,* 1906) and transcendental nature writing (*The Centaur,* 1911). As a writer of weird fiction, he belongs to a tradition of horror literature and ghost stories developed by Victorian writers such as Sheridan Le Fanu, R.L. Stevenson, Oscar Wilde, Sir Arthur Conan Doyle, M.R. James, E.F. Benson and others.

Although Blackwood loathed life in the city, he spent long periods both in New York and London, whether by choice or compulsion. In his autobiographical account of his youth, *Episodes Before Thirty,* Blackwood describes the ravishing effects of city-life on his mind and character: "I seemed covered with sore and tender places into which New York rubbed salt and acid every hour of the day" (124).

Blackwood's urban existence stood in sharp contrast with a particular kind of nature mysticism which he developed at an early age:

Bringing comfort, companionship, inspiration, joy, the spell of Nature has remained dominant, a truly magical spell ... The early feeling that everything was alive, a dim sense that some kind of consciousness struggled through every form, even that a sort of inarticulate communication with this "other life" was possible, could I but discover the way—these moods coloured its opening wonder. (Blackwood, *Episodes Before Thirty* 32–33)

For Blackwood, nature acted as an antithesis to the materialistic reality centered on personal profit (Joshi, *Unutterable Horror* 380–381); a sort of natural theology that not only runs through much Romantic writing a hundred years earlier, but which was also underpinned by the theories of the German philosopher Gustav Fechner, who expressed the idea that everything in the Universe had a soul[9] (Ashley 24). Blackwood travelled far and wide in search of intimate experiences of nature that would set him on the path to a deeper illumination, and transformed many of his experiences into stories set in more or less exotic locations.[10]

However, Blackwood also used England as the setting for tales in which nature provides transcendence and a consciousness of a more profound reality. One of these is the short story "The Man Whom the Trees Loved", set on the borders of the New Forest. In this novella, the contrast between the familiar English landscape and the unknown, fearsome reality that lurks just beyond its borders, makes it more poignant than most of his other tales. The story is mainly about escaping from a trivial reality into a deeper, more fulfilling world in which the natural and the supernatural converge. The protagonist, David Bittacy, has developed an almost mystical relationship with trees during his many years as a civil servant in India, and once retired to a villa in the New Forest, the English trees beckon him to join them in a mysterious communion that his wife can't understand, but which attracts him profoundly:

She saw him go away from her, go of his own accord and willingly beyond her; she saw the branches drop about his steps and hide him. His figure faded out among

---

9   In turn, Gustav Fechner (1881–1887) based his theories on the German Romantic idea of *Naturphilosophie*.

10   Among others, "The Wendigo", which takes place in the Canadian wilderness where Blackwood went moose-hunting in 1898; "The Glimmer of the Snow", set in the Swiss Alps where Blackwood would spend countless winter seasons up to the very end of his life; "Sand", an imaginative reflection of his experiences in Egypt; "The Willows", based on a canoe trip undertaken with a friend on the Danube, and the mystical autobiographical novel *The Centaur*, which imaginatively chronicles his travels in the Caucasus.

the speckled shade and sunlight. The trees covered him. The tide just took him, all unresisting and content to go … Beyond this stealthy silence, just within the edge of it, the things of another world were passing … It seemed that behind and through the glare of this wintry noonday in the heart of the woods there brooded another universe of life and passion, for her all unexpressed. The silence veiled it, the stillness hid it; but he moved with it all and understood. (261–262)

In the story, Bittacy takes on the role of an explorer of the liminal space between the natural and the supernatural, mediated by the trees. However, not all trees are the same; Bittacy has planted a cedar in his garden, and the English trees rage against it. Eventually the cedar is uprooted and destroyed in a storm that, the narrator hints, is prompted by the angry spirits of the native woods. In this, "The Man Whom the Trees Loved" reflects a typically Edwardian desire to purge the autochthonous of foreign influences and retrieve older and more authentic traditions in the face of contemporary threats, such as the growing rivalry with Germany in trade and armament. The setting is surely no coincidence: the New Forest is a place with a special role in the English imagination, haunted by legends since time immemorial and subjected to foreign rule when William the Conqueror restrained public access to the forest and turned it into a royal hunting reserve for the Norman elite.

A third important contributor to this type of literature was the Welsh writer Arthur Machen, who grew up in the village of Caerleon, surrounded by forests, hills and old Roman forts. This environment, imbued with history and myth, would have a strong hold on Machen's imagination throughout his life, and in his works he would refer to the area as Gwent,[11] the name of the corresponding medieval Welsh kingdom. The attitude is clearly reminiscent of the regional world-building also present in Thomas's "South Country", in so far as Machen, in his literary intercourse with the natural world of his native county, strives to unearth older, half-buried cultural strata in which the natural and the supernatural mix uncannily.

---

11   As he notes in his autobiography *Far Off Things*, his work "had all been the expression of one formula, one endeavour. What I had been doing is this; I had been inventing tales in which and by which I had tried to realise my boyish impressions of that wonderful magic Gwent" (19).

As a young man, Machen went to London to study and to establish himself as a writer. Like Thomas and Blackwood, he loathed the city, which seemed to drain him of energy, but even so he could still perceive its underlying depths, especially during his long nightly walks, when the dreary everyday reality of London was transformed into something shining and fantastic.[12] He would return to the fascination he felt for such transformations—Machen referred to them as "transmutations"—time and again in his writings, from the autobiographical *Hill of Dreams* (1907) to the later reminiscences in the novella *A Fragment of Life* (1906) and *Far Off Things* (1922).

Machen combined his career as a journalist with the writing of weird tales, the subject matter of which frequently involved occult rituals[13] and the presence of ancient mythical creatures lingering just below the surface of everyday reality. In the First World War Machen worked as a war correspondent for the *Evening News* and became famous for his story "The Bowmen", published in 1914, about an army of ghosts of medieval British bowmen which appears out of nowhere to succour the beleagered British soldiers who were trapped during the Battle of Mons in August, 1914.[14]

In his most successful stories, however, Machen moves away from the overtly supernatural and enters a liminal area which blends nature, cultural memory and imagination, to explore the interaction between these deeper dimensions of the landscape and the everyday Edwardian reality of his characters. His native town, where the old Roman remains mingled with the autochthonous Celtic and Welsh heritage, provided subject matter for many of these stories, which were set off and given shape by local nature. One example is the first chapter of Machen's

---

12 These explorations rightly earned Machen the status of a pioneer of what has later been labelled "psychogeography". See Coverley, especially chapter 1.

13 Like Blackwood, Machen joined the *Order of the Golden Dawn* and experimented with occultism; reportedly the two writers met and got on well enough, but didn't much enjoy each other's writings (Ashley 113–114).

14 In spite of its ostensibly supernatural content, the story was taken as a real news report by many, in spite of Machen's later insistence that it was merely a product of his own imagination (Joshi, "Introduction" *xxi)*. If nothing else, the reception of the story testifies to the willingness of the British to believe in miracles and supernatural intervention in the years of the Great War.

autobiographical novel *Hill of Dreams*, written between 1895 and 1897, but not published until 1907, in which the dreamy protagonist and aspiring writer Lucian—a thinly disguised Machen—is suddenly struck by the transformative powers of the landscape. As Lucian leaves his house to go for a walk at dusk, nature seems to conspire with his consciousness of the lingering presence of a much older past, the attunement to which endows him with a transcendental perception of the world.

> As Lucian looked, he was amazed, as though he were reading a wonderful story, the meaning of which was a little greater than his understanding. Then, like the hero of a fairy-book, he went on and on, catching now and again glimpses of the amazing country into which he had penetrated, and perceiving rather than seeing that as the day waned everything grew more grey and somber ... He walked smartly down the hill; the air was all glimmering and indistinct, transmuting trees and hedges into ghostly shapes ... He liked history, but he loved to meditate on a land laid waste, Britain deserted by the legions, the rare pavements riven by frost, Celtic magic still brooding on the wild hills and in the black depths of the forest. (65–66)

The Hill of Dreams ends in tragedy, when the main character is forced to leave his native Welsh village for London, where he attempts to conjure up the same experience but is left exhausted, overwhelmed by a city that forces itself upon his perception in unwanted ways and finally prompts him to commit suicide. To some extent, it reflects Machen's own early experiences in London, but as opposed to his semi-fictional hero, Machen learned to come to terms with the city, and would revisit the plot of *The Hill of Dreams* later in life. The novella *A Fragment of Life* (1906) is, again, a story of a Welshman trapped by bourgeoise conventions in the city of London, but this time Machen allows his protagonist the possibility of redemption. Edward Darnell (again, in all likelihood, modelled on Machen himself) rediscovers the allure of the country after many years in the city—and he does so by reenacting his youthful walks, which now take him out of the thronged city centre and into a suburbia where the country and the city suggestively blend and create visions of supernatural marvels:

> There was a rapture in Darnell's voice as he spoke, that made his story well-nigh swell into a song, and he drew a long breath as the words ended, filled with the thought of that far-off summer day, when some enchantment had informed all common things, transmuting them into a great sacrament, causing earthly works

to glow with the fire and the glory of the everlasting light ... I would roam about old, dim squares and hear the wind whispering in the trees ... The shadow, and the dim lights, and the cool of the evening, and the trees that were like dark low clouds were all mine, and mine alone ... I was living in a world that nobody else knew of, into which no one could enter. (183)

The novella culminates with the couple's decision to move back to Darnell's old family home in Wales, to be enriched by the landscape and all that it contains in terms of cultural and mythical heritage, without yielding either to mad escapism or to a crude obliteration of such legacies. The concluding lines consist of an annotation by Darnell, which shows the rich blend of fantasy and reality that informs this natural space, charged with tradition and mystery:

So I awoke from a dream of a London suburb, of daily labour, of weary, useless little things; and as my eyes were opened I saw that I was in an ancient wood, where a clear well rose into a grey film and vapour beneath a misty, glimmering heat. And a form came towards me from the hidden places of the wood, and my love and I were united by the well. (222)

Collectively, Thomas, Blackwell and Machen portray the English countryside not only as a site of consolation, recreation and escape from a dreary city-life, but also a catalyst for ancient myth, the supernatural and horror, giving expression to inherently Edwardian tensions that would culminate in the Great War only a few years ahead.

Post-Edwardian rural fantasy narratives

Whereas the First World War famously did away with fairies, superstition and old traditions for many modernist writers,[15] nature remained a source of relief throughout the years of the war, even in the trenches (as John Lewis-Stempel amply demonstrates in his study *Where Poppies*

---

15   Garth discusses this at some length in his biographical study *Tolkien and the Great War*, especially in the chapter "Postscript. One who Dreams Alone" (2004, 287–313).

Blow), and other writers remained attached to the old traditions. Spiritism, which became very popular in the years after the war, allowed an outlet for people who could not believe in conventional religion after the war, but who did believe in the possibility of communicating with the spirits of the many dead sons, brothers, fiancés and friends who had been torn from the prime of life so suddenly. Conan Doyle is but one famous example of converts in this field, whose new faith in the existence of spirits—and, in Conan Doyle's case, even in fairies—would yield very public statements concerning the actual value of such anti-rationalist approaches to reality.[16] In literature, established writers like Walter de la Mare, John Masefield and H.G. Wells would perpetuate supernatural and speculative modes of fiction, and a strain of fantasy that involved encounters with faries and/or elves in transcendental regions, set off by a quiet and close observation of secluded, twilit natural spaces, also emerged as a type of story derived from the original fairy tales of German Romanticism (which found its British version mainly in the mentioned works of George MacDonald), and the pseudo-medieval prose romances of William Morris, which have already been discussed. Novels such as E.R. Eddison's *The Worm Ouroborous* (1922), Lord Dunsany's *The King of Elfland's Daughter* (1924), and Hope Mirrlee's *Lud-in the Mist* (1926) were instrumental in giving shape to this new type of fantasy tale. The following is a scene from Dunsany's novel that well shows its indebtedness to the mentioned traditions:

> By the time the sun set he would be standing quiet by a hedge that ran right down to the frontier of twilight ... and the pigeons would come home to trees of the fields we know, and twittering starlings; and the elfin horns would blow, clear silver magical music thrilling the chilled air, and all the colours of clouds would go suddenly changing; it was then in the failing light, in the darkening of colours, that Orion would watch for a dim white shape stepping out of the border of twilight. And this evening, just as he hushed a hound with his hand, just as our fields went dim, there slipped a great white unicorn out of the border, still munching lilies such as never grew in any field of ours. (Dunsany 125)

The literary works we have studied in the present chapter make it clear that in the Edwardian period, the Romantic impulse which had been

---

16 As shown by the famous case of the photographs of the "Cottingley fairies", the authenticity of which was defended by Conan Doyle.

present in Victorian literature through original fairy tales, pseudo-medieval prose romances, neo-Gothic tales of horror, adventure stories and a blend of nature writing and fantasy, merged and warped into the type of literature that readers of modern fantasy would recognize today. Nature here acted as a transcendental, liminal space that offered imaginative possibilities and served as a counter-narrative that engaged obliquely with a disenchanted contemporary reality. However, it would be impossible to properly understand and assess the role nature played in the emergence of modern fantasy—and consequently the type of discourse that Ursula K. Le Guin would modify and alter so decisively in her books of Earthsea—without looking at the contribution of J.R.R. Tolkien to this field.

III J.R.R. Tolkien's Depiction of Nature

J.R.R. Tolkien is the most famous example of a war-veteran who refused to say "good-bye to all that"—to use the famous title of Graves' 1929 autobiography—and took to writing fantasy narratives that, like the predecessors we have just discussed, provide the reader with visions of wonder set off by nature, in order to reenchant a dreary contemporary reality.

Tolkien's most famous works of fantasy, *The Hobbit*, *The Lord of the Rings* and *The Silmarillion*, were not published until 1937, 1954–55 and 1977 respectively, but he had begun writing sustained narratives of fantasy as early as 1917. Two different moments related to intimate experiences of nature, beauty and transcendence—one just before the outbreak of the war, and the other soon after Tolkien's return from the Somme—frame his descent into the infernal reality of the trenches, and the three experiences together were crucial in setting off his particular creativity.

The first moment took place in Cornwall, in August of 1914. As John Garth explains, Tolkien was sitting on the very edge of the Lizard Peninsula, the south-westernmost point of Britain, watching the rise of Venus, the evening star. The moment was enhanced by a reading of a poem in Old English that Tolkien had come across a few years earlier: *Crist II*, by Cynewulf, which speaks mysteriously of a certain Earendel as being "the brighest of angels", a divine personification of the evening star, "sent over Middle-earth". Tolkien asked himself where this Earendel might have come from, and looking into the West at the star on that evening in August, 1914, Garth argues that the experience set off a vision in Tolkien's mind which found its creative outlet in a poem he wrote a few months later, "The Voyage of Éarendel the Evening Star" (*The Worlds of J.R.R. Tolkien*, 64). This poem was the first expression of Middle-earth, which was to become the most famous literary fantasy world of the 20th century.

The next experience was Tolkien's participation in the Great War. Here some background is needed to understand what the war meant to

Tolkien in terms of loss and recovery. Tolkien had grown up with the fairy tales and legends compiled by Andrew Lang, and he had been exposed to the nature of the countryside just outside Birmingham in his formative years, where he played and walked, climbed trees and picked mushrooms with his brother Hilary (Carpenter 28–29). He had a fascination for older forms of culture, literature, art and nature, partly inculcated by his move from the arid High Veldt of South Africa to the lush green country hamlet of Sarehole as a four-year-old in 1896, partly because of a natural talent for languages and etymology, but also due to his mother's conversion to Catholicism and a keen interest in botany (Carpenter 30). The "homecoming" to a natural paradise would soon be associated with a sense of loss when the family moved to the heavily industrialized city of Birmingham, which was followed by a still greater loss—the death of his mother—which left Tolkien and his brother orphaned and forced to live in a series of boarding-houses under the tutelage of a Catholic priest. Tolkien sought to replace these losses by actively recapturing the spirit of the old through his study of ancient literature and old languages, and through debates on art and modernity with a group of like-minded friends.[17] Another source of relief was his wife, Edith Bratt, also an orphan living in one of the Birmingham boarding houses to which the brothers had been sent. Tolkien moved to Oxford in 1911, and in 1916 he finished his degree in the discipline he most cherished, Old and Middle English. He was well on his way towards an academic career in philology when the war, which had broken out two years before, threatened to obliterate everything he had fought so hard to achieve.

The Great War famously provided a sort of anti-thesis to the English countryside, articulated by the infernal sceneries of the frontline, with its ravished No Man's Land where the artillery had turned the formerly green landscapes into a mud field full of oozing craters and broken stumps of trees.[18] On the Somme, Tolkien himself received his share of

---

17   Garth (2004) discusses at length Tolkien's engagement with (and the impact of) the ideas of the other members of the so-called TCBS (Tea Club and Barrovian Society), an informal club he had formed with his friends from King Edward's School in Birmingham.

18   Paul Fussell devotes a chapter ('Arcadian Recourses') in his seminal study *The Great War and Modern Memory* to the effects of such landscapes on the British

the most devastating effects of modern technology and the brutal mind-sets of modernity. As a direct effect of the War, he lost two of his closest friends and became an invalid for a protracted period of time. The experience consolidated his distaste for industrialized modernity and machines, and made him even more bent on recovering the old and eternal in literature, something which he felt was quite beyond the sorrows of life in the mortal world, of which he had seen so much already.[19] More importantly, Tolkien's experiences in the trenches set off his creativity.

The second moment that framed Tolkien's experiences of the war, and provided a decisive thrust forward in his career as a mythopoeic writer, took place in a clearing in an English wood in 1917. After participating in the Battle of the Somme, Tolkien was recovering from trench fever at Roos, in Yorkshire. Edith had joined him there, and danced for Tolkien in a glade full of white flowers. For Tolkien, the vision must have provided a counterpoint to the infernal sceneries he had witnessed first hand in France less than a year earlier, and just as the vision of the trenches had sparked *The Fall of Gondolin* during the winter of 1916–17, the experience in the woods became the origin of the *Tale of Beren and Luthien* (the second "Great Tale" of *The Silmarillion*, together with *The Fall of Gondolin* and *The Children of Húrin*, which tell of the adventures of Elves and Men in the First Age of Middle-earth).

The two moments of intimacy in an ostensibly English natural environment, together with Tolkien's experiences in the war, acted upon his imagination both antithetically and sympathetically, and together with his already extensive knowledge of native myths and legends, helped him articulate his own literary vision, that would become the single strongest impact on twentieth-century fantasy fiction.

In terms of the representation of the natural world in Tolkien's works, much has been said already,[20] and I will here limit the discussion to a few examples of how his literature provides a synthesis of the Edwardian

---

soldiers' imagination, in turn heavily informed by extensive readings of pastoral poetry.

19   For a more thorough analysis of Tolkien's emotional and aesthetic response to the First World War, see Garth, *Tolkien and the Great War* (especially 287–313).

20   See, for example Campbell, Dickerson and Evans, Jeffers, and Simonson 2015.

merging of nature and fantasy that we have outlined in the previous chapter. One the one hand, it is true that, after the war, Tolkien gave up his early flirtation with the Edwardian fairy-tradition, and instead of portrayals of flimsy, ethereal creatures in poems such as 'Goblin Feet', he developed a different kind of fairies. Tolkien's Elves, Dwarves and Orcs are not only larger, but also far more serious than their Edwardian predecessors, and this solemnity is closer to, say, Lord Dunsany's portrayal of Elfland in *The King of Elfland's Daughter*. In that respect, the war *did* do away with some of the more innocent and frivolous notions of fairies that the Edwardians had been so infatuated with. On a larger scale, however, Tolkien echoes many of the preceding Edwardian expressions in his portrayal of nature. For one thing, in *The Hobbit* and *The Lord of the Rings*, Tolkien favours country over city, agriculture over industry, the simplicity of a rural lifestyle over the sophistication of urban life. His forceful rejection of machines and modern technology is aligned with the Edwardian recovery of the rural (but also enhanced and modified by his experiences in the Great War). As for his anti-commercialism, it was at least in part inspired by the Arts and Crafts movement, of which William Morris, a great inspiration for Tolkien (Carpenter 77–78), had been one of the most eloquent proponents.

Tolkien thus equated the idea of England with the sense of a homecoming, and that homecoming was to a green rural world, in which the landscape was imbued with myth, coloured by history. Like Kipling's children's stories in which Dan and Una revisit British semi-legendary history through their encounter with Puck in a secluded English woodland valley,[21] or when Mole of *The Wind in the Willows* loses his way in the Wild Woods but finds relief in Badger's homely underground dwelling, the hobbit protagonists of *The Hobbit* and *The Lord of the Rings*, child-like in their innocent view of the larger world and their own role in History, likewise meet ancient beings that dwell on the borders of their own comfortable countryside dwelling. These encounters put things in perspective and allow the hobbits to delve deeper into their own history, from which they have become detached by custom and complacency,

---

21   Kipling himself was born in the colonies and "discovered" the marvels England at roughly the same time as Tolkien, but as an adult.

living, as they do, in a modern world with post offices and butcher's shops; in Tolkien's own words, a fictionalised version of England in the times of the "Diamond Jubilee" (Tolkien, *Letters* 230).

In *The Hobbit*, the bourgeoise country squire Bilbo[22] is visited by Gandalf, who reminds him that he still has a "passport into the ancient world" (Shippey 72). Bilbo leaves the known world behind and sets out on an adventure, ostensibly to assist in a treasure hunt, but also very clearly in search of the wide world itself (Lobdell 16), and of his own role in it. The experiences prompt Bilbo to reassess his own identity, and enrich his understanding of his place in the wider context of things through exposure to deeper layers of history and myth. On one level, the adventures of Bilbo thus recall the Edwardian adventure novels of Englishmen on expeditions and quests in far corners of the Empire, but on a deeper level, his journey "There and Back Again" is about more profound discoveries concerning the value of the natural world as a mediator of transcendence. However, *The Hobbit* was only a trial of a more thorough exploration of these themes that Tolkien engaged in while writing *The Lord of the Rings*.

In the more mature version of Middle-earth that is articulated in the latter work, nature, history and legends blend freely—as they do in Edward Thomas's "Home" from the mentioned collection *Rest and Unrest*, in which a young soldier is dying and recalls a childhood visit to Wales with his father, where the countryside turns into an enchanted place imbued with myth and legends. In *The Lord of the Rings*, Frodo sets out with three friends, leaving behind the known, rural world of The Shire with a Ring that must be destroyed. While the scheme of the treasure hunt of *The Hobbit* is thus inverted—this adventure is about getting rid of a treasure, not finding one—the essence of the adventure remains, and the four hobbits soon find themselves entering the Old Forest to escape from the threat of their persecutors. In this liminal space, on the very borders of the known world, the trees do not provide solace, but represent a threat. Nature takes on a sublime dimension mixing wonder and terror, and the forest is pictured as an old home to which the hobbits no longer belong completely—in fact, they have

---

22   See chapter 3 in Shippey.

actively hedged it out from their fields—and which might just destroy them if they are not careful. The forest here recalls Blackwood's portrayal of the active and awe-inspiring trees in "The Willows", but more importantly the depiction in "The Man Whom the Trees Loved", where the woods simultaneously take on the role of a home for the initiated, and a threat for those who have become too detached from it to appreciate its intrinsic and native value. In the novel *The Hill of Dreams*, Machen's depiction of the main character Lucian's sense of awe as the light changes and he becomes aware of the mythical depths and terrors of the forest right around the corner from his Welsh home, is also similar to the hobbits' sense of awe and terror in the Old Forest, but the parallel to Mole's adventure in the Wild Woods, in *The Wind in the Willows*, is perhaps the strongest.[23]

Just when Old Man Willow has enchanted the hobbits and all seems lost, Tom Bombadil, ancient as the hills, comes by to liberate them and takes them to his home. Likewise, Mole, after having lost his way in the terrifying woods (which he enters freely in search of an adventure), ends up inside a hollow tree, and is saved by Badger, who welcomes him into his warm, safe and cosy home. Badger and Tom Bombadil are examples of the old order, beings who are somehow immune to the malign influence of the forest, in which they both dwell peacefully—Tom with roots reaching back to the beginning of time, and Badger, said to be the oldest animal to inhabit the British Isles, dwelling in a house whose cellars and tunnels are riddled with Roman remains. The two episodes represent the idea of a homecoming to a safe, snug, simple and healthy rural retreat, and serve as a reward for the audacious explorations of the protagonists, who come away enriched by their intimacies with the deeper historical and mythical dimensions of their native lands.

Coupled with this exploration is an exposure to the sublime forces of nature, which causes fear and apprehension. The combination is at the core of Tolkien's vision of what he called the "Perilous Land" (Tolkien, *Tolkien Reader* 33). Faëry is a dangerous territory insofar as it puts things in perspective: the "Perilous Realm" shows us that the world is larger than we thought (and we are smaller), unveiling both our

---

23   For a fuller analysis of this correspondence, see Cossio (2020).

connection to and estrangement from this reality. The hobbits' growing fear of the trees in the Old Forest; their terror as Old Man Willow threatens to kill them; the primal Gothic horror of being abducted by the spectral Barrow Wights on the Barrow Downs (on the very borders of the familiar world); Pippin and Merry's initial fear of the intimidating Treebeard, and Smith's terror of the raging storm and the marching Elves in *Smith of Wootton Major*, are all examples of the Edwardian version of the Romantic sublime, in which modern Englishmen probe the historical, mythical and cultural depths of homelike regions, and occasionally discover that the native woods hold mysteries too strong for them.

In narrative terms, the transitions from the known and trivial reality are set off by changing light, fog, shadows, storms and murky environments that affect the characters' "normal" vision of the known world. As in Edward Thomas' and Arthur Machen's stories, nature itself and the characters' perception of it are of equal importance when assessing and interpreting the imaginative possibilities of such spaces, as shown in the episodes of Thomas's *The South Country*, and "The Queen of the Waste Lands", or Machen's *The Hill of Dreams* or *A Fragment of Life* that we discussed above. Verlyn Flieger has argued that the hobbits' subjective *interpretation* of what occurs in the Old Forest is key to the reader's understanding of the episode ("Faërie: Tolkien's Perilous Realm" 40). If so, this perception is affected by an imaginative vision—enhanced in turn by legends and history—and of the natural environment itself. Merry, who lives near the Old Forest and is familiar with it from personal experience, from the tales and legends told about it, and from historical references to previous events, tells the other hobbits what he knows, and leaves it to them to ascertain whether or not the stories are true. In this way, nature, myth and history interact with the imagination, as in the Edwardian explorations of the liminal space on the very borders of our known reality.

Such explorations frequently involve transcendental experiences, of which examples abound in Edwardian literature. In Blackwood's story, set in the New Forest, David Bittacy achieves a higher communion with the trees and merges uncannily with their native arboreal world, disappearing into its mysteries. Machen's story of a married couple's trivial life in London transitions into a return to a deeper reality of the main character's native Wales, shaped by legends, a heightened perception, and by local nature itself. Thomas's vision of the Queen of the Wastelands is triggered by a vision of a valley from a high place, with hilltops like islands in the clouds, imaginatively enhanced by a knowledge of folktales and myth. In Tolkien's work, the episodes in Tom Bombadil's house and in the barrows are both preceded by transitions into worlds where an altered state of awareness prevails, allowing for transcendental experiences (Simonson, "Out of this World"). In the house of Tom Bombadil, the hobbits break through to a different realm, separated from conventional notions and measurements of space and time, where they enter into communion with nature itself, shaped by the legends and stories Tom tells them, which take them on paths of the imagination to a higher, less prosaic reality. When Tom saves them from the Barrow–wights, a shaken Merry awakes from a vision of the ancient reality in which the buried kings once dwelled, as real to him as if he had actually experienced it (Tolkien, *Lord of the Rings* 156). The whole episode takes on an almost symbolic quality which is emblematic of the Edwardian narratives we have discussed, but also of Lord Dunsany's post-war rendering of such transcendental experiences.

Tolkien's 1967 story *Smith of Wootton Major* is an even clearer example of his take on the Edwardian experience of nature, myth and imagination. The main character Smith, having swallowed a magic star from Faery as a child, is enriched by the imaginative and creative possibilities it offers him, and uses the star as a passport to leave his native Wootton Major and enter Faery through the gateway of the forest, which acts as a liminal space. Here he meets the Queen of Faery, but she makes it clear to him that he can't stay in this transcendental world of heightened perception forever (Tolkien, *Smith* 33). Just like Alveric of Lord Dunsany's tale "loses" his capacity to cross the threshold of twilight and enter Elfland as he grows older (while his son Orion has inherited the capacity), Smith is forced to leave Faery behind, and yield the star to a new generation of children. The star becomes a symbol of the gift of perception of this higher reality, which sets off imagination, awareness and creativity, and makes life richer for others.

Tolkien's "Recovery" and transcendentalism[24]

We have seen that Tolkien's depiction of nature reflects an Edwardian strain of literary transcendentalism, to which he was exposed in life and literature as a child. Naturally, neither Tolkien nor the Edwardians invented the concept of transcendentalism, and here I wish to trace its roots to American transcendentalism, and further back, and give some examples of how Tolkien, inspired by the Edwardian literature we have discussed, makes this fundamentally Romantic imperative available to contemporary readers.

Tolkien himself theorized about literary explorations of the higher realities (that he called Faëry) in his seminal essay "On Fairy Stories", speaking of Secondary Worlds that we can enter through the literary craft of the story teller, a sort of "Elvish enchantment" which allows the reader to escape from a trivial and dreary unimaginative reality, recover the childlike wonder and appreciation of the natural and imaginative marvels of the world, and be consoled by the experience.

Of the three main concepts, "Escape", "Recovery" and "Consolation" (Tolkien 1966), I will focus here on Tolkien's ideas concerning "recovery" and wonder through experiences of nature and fairy tales, which he articulated in "On Fairy Stories". As mentioned, this notion is informed by the Romantic tradition, but also by Edwardian literary renderings of American transcendentalism, expressed through nature-based fantasy works, in which an active imaginative engagement with the multiple dimensions of place allows for transcendence—momentary, transient or more lasting.

Tolkien's (1966:77) view of the concept is that

> we need recovery. We should look at green again, and be startled anew (but not blinded) by blue and yellow and red. We should meet the centaur and the dragon, and then perhaps suddenly behold, like the ancient shepherds, sheep, and dogs,

---

24 Parts of this section have been adapted from Simonson's "Recovering the Utterly Alien Land: Tolkien and Transcendentalism", in Segura, Eduardo and Thomas Honegger (eds.), *Myth and magic: Art According to the Inklings*, Zurich & Jena: Walking Tree Publishers, 2006.

and horses—and wolves. This recovery fairy-stories help us to make. In that sense
only a taste for them may make us, or keep us, childish.

> Recovery (which includes return and renewal of health) is a regaining of a clear
> view . . . We need, in any case, to clean our windows; so that the things seen clearly
> may be freed from the drab blur of triteness or familiarity—from possessiveness.

When Tolkien laid out these ideas, he partly echoed a long tradition of
pagan and Christian Neoplatonic philosophy that addressed the question
of how fallen man might be able to recover contact with Nature. Plotinus,
in his *Enneads*, conceived the problem as the overflowing of a spring
that, when the flow reaches the material world, has come so far from
its divine source that Evil occurs. Neoplatonised Christianity in general
regarded the fall of man as a falling away from Oneness, as represented
by God, into a fragmented state of multiplicity. Hence, redemption was
seen as a process of reintegration. For Plotinus, the solution lay in looking inward, toward the essence of things, while Neoplatonised Christianity postulated the existence of a powerful current of love sent out by
God to transport us back to Him.

The idea that multiplicity leads to Evil was also present in much of
German idealism. As Abrams explains, from the 1780's on,

> a number of the keenest and most sensitive minds found radically inadequate,
> both to immediate human experience and to basic human needs, the intellectual
> ambiance of the Enlightenment, with (as they saw it) its mechanistic world-view,
> its analytic divisiveness (which undertook to explain all physical and mental phe-
> nomena by breaking them down into irreducible parts, and regarded all wholes as
> a collocation of such elementary parts), and its conception of the human mind as
> totally diverse and alien from its nonmental environment. (170–171)

Transcendental idealism, as expressed by Schelling and others, held that
imagination was the key that enabled us to conceive of, and reconcile,
contradictions, thus leading us back towards a unity with Nature. The
Romantic stance was a variation upon the theme of original Oneness as
equated with Goodness, while multiplicity implied a fall into evil and
suffering that Man must overcome. In the Romantic mind frame, the
"return to unity is not a return to undifferentiated unity of its origin,
but a unity which is higher, because it incorporates the intervening differentiations" (Abrams 183–184). For the Romantics, imagination was a

tool that could be used to help us move in this direction—an enhanced awareness of reality.

In Coleridge's opinion, taken from *Biographia Literaria* (1817), custom is what prevents us from seeing clearly, and the trademark of poetic genius is to be able to describe "familiar objects as to awaken in the mind of others a kindred feeling concerning them and that freshness of sensation which is the constant accompaniment of mental, no less than of bodily, convalescence" (Coleridge 60). A similar view is found in Carlyle's *Sartor Resartus* (1830–31), in which the author expresses the idea that custom blinds us to the miracles of the everyday by "persuading us that the Miraculous, by simple repetition, ceases to be Miraculous" (Trilling and Bloom 34). Carlyle asks himself: "Am I to view the stupendous with stupid indifference, because I have seen it twice, or two-hundred, or two-million times?" (35)

The American philosopher Ralph Waldo Emerson made Carlyle's work known in the United States, and incorporated much of his thinking, largely derived from the Romantics, in what became known as the transcendentalist movement, of which he was one of the founders. As Emerson wrote in 'The Transcendentalist' (1841–42), transcendentalism was really idealism, one of the two main outlooks upon life, the other being materialism. The difference, according to Emerson, is that "the materialist insists on facts, on history, on the force of circumstances and the animal wants of man; the idealist on the power of Thought and Will, on inspiration, on miracle, on individual culture" (81).

One of the most influential essays written by Emerson is "Nature" (1836), which came to be considered the manifesto of the transcendentalist movement. Early on, Emerson states what he perceives to be one of the fundamental problems of Man:

> To speak truly, few adult persons can see nature. Most persons do not see the sun. At least they have a very superficial seeing. The sun illuminates only the eye of the man, but shines into the eye and the heart of the child. The lover of nature is he whose inward and outward senses are still truly adjusted to each other; who has retained the spirit of infancy even into the era of manhood. (6)

Emerson, too, believes that man has fallen away from the original oneness, and that only as children we are able to perceive the world as it is, as unity. To adjust the inward and outward senses is to see oneself as part of the original unity. Evidence of man's fall would be our present estrangement from Nature: "We are as much strangers in nature as we are aliens from God. We do not understand the note of birds. The fox and the deer run away from us; the bear and tiger rend us" (33). Like Coleridge and Carlyle, he identifies custom as one of the main obstacles for perceiving the miraculous in the everyday, and claims that the duty of the writer is to "fasten words again to visible things; so that picturesque language is at once a commanding certificate that he who employs it is a man in alliance with truth and God" (16).

In Emerson's view, language itself has become an obstacle for our perception of God in nature, and the task of the writer is to find the words to penetrate the veil of familiarity and enable us see our original relation to God and the world that surrounds us, as Oneness. This act, according to Emerson, is the will of God, because "good writing and brilliant discourse are perpetual allegories. This imagery is spontaneous. It is the blending of experience with the present action of the mind. It is proper creation. It is the working of the original Cause through the instruments he has already made" (16).

These ideas not only recall Tolkien's belief that we must return to a childlike perception of reality to be able to grasp the miracle of everyday phenomena (the writing and reading of fairy-stories is Tolkien's particular way of "adjusting the inward and outward senses"), but also that good story-telling partly aims to recover an original relationship with the natural world,[25] and that "sub-creation" is an act of allegiance with God.[26]

---

25   When discussing the desire to talk to beasts that can be found in many fairy-stories, Tolkien uses an analogy not much different from Emerson's, claiming that such a desire is not due to "an alleged 'absence of the sense of separation of ourselves to the beasts'", but rather the contrary: "A vivid sense of that separation is very ancient; but also a sense that it was a severance: a strange fate and a guilt lies on us. Other creatures are like other realms with which Man has broken off relations, and sees now only from the outside at a distance, being at war with them, or on the terms of an uneasy armistice" (1966, 84).

26   In *Mythopoeia*, Tolkien justifies the fantastical elements of fairy-stories by asserting that sub-creation is a God-given right: "Though all the crannies of the world we filled/With Elves and Goblins, though we dared to build/Gods and their houses out of dark and light,/and sowed the seed of dragons—'twas our right/(used or misused). That right has not decayed:/we make still by the law in which we're made". Qtd. in Flieger (*Splintered Light* 42–43).

Emerson further implies that the intuitive and spontaneous use of the right words for the natural objects they represent is a speech-act in the sense that it creates the world it describes, making it visible to the reader.

Tolkien, writing in a time and a place in which the natural environment had been long-since defiled, turned into a commodity or contemplated as mere space on a map that must be conquered by technology, trade and warfare, would mainly look to the Northwest of the past for inspiration, but his vision was also rooted in Neoplatonic, Romantic, and Transcendentalist thinking, filtered by the fundamentally Edwardian literary expressions we have just discussed. The notion of Recovery and the inhibiting effects of custom clearly repeat—indeed almost paraphrase—the words of Coleridge, Carlyle and Emerson, and the idea of the writer as a subcreator was explicit in Emerson's writings, as we have seen. Likewise, Owen Barfield's conception of words and their semantic unity with the natural and supernatural world, which had a profound influence on Tolkien,[27] was preceded by Thoreau's elaboration on the same theme and partly inherited by Neoplatonised Christianity and Romantic thought, as we can appreciate in Flieger's summary of Barfield's theory:

> Language in its beginnings made no distinction between the literal and the metaphoric meaning of a word, as it does today ... Humankind in its beginnings had a sense of the cosmos as a whole and of itself as a part of that whole ... We now perceive the cosmos as particularized, fragmented, and entirely separate from ourselves. Our consciousness and the language with which we express that consciousness have changed and splintered. (*Splintered Light* 37–38)

For Barfield and Tolkien, as for Emerson and Thoreau, words were the tools we must use to bridge the gap and recover unity. As Flieger points out,

> *Poetic Diction* makes it clear that it is in and by words that we feel and express a sense of separation and that it will be through the creative power of words that we can return. The poet, through the use of metaphor, is a maker of meaning and a recreator of perception. Poetry—poetic diction—reinvests the world with meaning and rebuilds our relationships with it. (*Splintered Light* 47–48)

---

27 For a full account of this influence, see Flieger's (2002) seminal study *Splintered Light*.

Indeed, transcendentalist philosophy in general seem to have been fore-runners to Tolkien in many senses. Of Thoreau's *A Week on the Concord and Merrimack Rivers*, Robinson says: "The book's probing of the relationship between Christianity and mythology, its critique of the narrowness of conventional society, its passionate concern with the dynamics of conversation and friendship, and its keen awareness of the natural world all reflect important strands of Transcendentalism" (53). The same words could have been used to describe *The Lord of the Rings*.

Is Tolkien, then, merely a twentieth-century echo of the Romantic and transcendentalist attempts at achieving Recovery through literature? The answer takes some pondering. Tolkien is clearly very much concerned with reinvesting words with original meaning, and, like the Romantics, he was not after a return to undifferentiated unity, but rather a "unity which is higher because it incorporates the intervening differentiations" (Abrams 183–184), as the words at the end of *On Fairy-stories* imply: "So great is the bounty with which [the Christian] has been treated ... that in Fantasy he may actually assist in the effoliation and multiple enrichment of creation" (Tolkien, *The Tolkien Reader* 89).

Tolkien similarly creates a world which is both familiar and strange at the same time, updating older words, traditions and world-visions by putting them in constant dialogue with more modern conceptions of reality, mainly represented by the hobbits. However, both Tolkien's point of departure and the refined process that leads up to the textual outcome is radically different from the Transcendentalists'. While Tolkien, like Thoreau, made use of old words to convey ancient realities, his words and languages were often invented, or semi-invented,[28] and they triggered the creation of imagined contexts to make them credible, albeit with clear links to "real" historical, cultural and literary contexts of our own world.

In a letter to his editor, Tolkien (*Letters* 219) explains that "The invention of languages is the foundation. The 'stories' were made rather to provide a world for the languages than the reverse. To me a name comes first and the story follows." One example of this is what happened to the pre-existing world of Middle-earth when the word 'hobbit' appeared in

---

28 *The Ring of Words* shows how Tolkien's work on the OED actually gave rise to many of his "invented" words.

his mind. In a note to the letter quoted above, Tolkien added: "I once scribbled 'hobbit' on a blank page of some boring school exam. paper in the early 1930's. It was some time before I discovered what it referred to!" (*Letters* 219)

Discovery of context by means of inventing linguistically credible etymologies was, for Tolkien, a crucial part of his particular creative labours.[29] In the case of the discovery of context for the word 'hobbit', the entry on this word in *The Ring of Words* explains that Tolkien came up with the non-existant but "well-formed Old English compound *holbytla*" (modern English hole-builder), later used by the Rohirrim to describe hobbits, as a result of 'reverse engineering': "Tolkien is playfully suggesting that if there had been an Old English word *holbytla* … it might well have come down into modern English as *hobbit*" (Gilliver et. al. 144–145).

Shippey's account of the word features an ample discussion of possible sources, mentioning the bourgeois Babbitt of Sinclair Lewis's eponymous novel as one possibility (acknowledged by Tolkien himself)—the story being, however vaguely, reminiscent of Bilbo's—and the word 'rabbit'. Both these sources and the reversed etymological engineering contribute to the fact that "'hobbit' as word and concept threw out its anchors into Old and modern English at once" (70).

The outcome of the process of creating a context for 'hobbit' is the Shire as portrayed in *The Lord of the Rings*; that is, a region that resembles modern England (or at least a version of a late nineteenth-century rural England), but with roots that reach back to earlier stages in Northern European history and culture, much like England's own.[30] However, the Shire is only one part of a much larger world, in which these earlier stages are still very much present and actively operating, such as Rohan (the context of *holbytlan*). Tolkien, in *The Lord of the Rings*, actually communicates a process of exploration and discovery of these ancient contexts by means of a fictitious chronicle known as 'The

---

29   Garbowski also highlights this feature as fundamental to Tolkien's process of creating a sense of recovery in his fiction: "If the artist were simply 'inventing' the world, then it would in part be the magic of control and domination he criticized" (80).

30   Shippey (*Road* 102) provides an outline of these correspondences.

Red Book of Westmarch', written by hobbits, who, by interpreting these older and more 'foreign' realities, make them accessible to the modern reader. The labouriously (though at the same time intuitively) wrought 'inter-traditional dialogue' that permeates all levels of the text (Simonson 2008) elucidates the relationship between the old and the new and conveys, at the same time, the underlying parallells to our own, present-day reality.

However, the process of taking the hobbits on a trip of discovery to increasingly archaic and unfamiliar settings involves not only reversed etymological engineering. For one thing, between the word and the world come the maps. Though the same impulse was to be found in *The Hobbit*—see Tolkien's claim that after having discovered the word 'hobbit', "I did nothing about it, for a long time, and for some years I got no further than the production of Thror's map" (*Letters* 215)—the map that appears in the earlier narrative was, as Shippey (100) points out, merely decorative. It was when Tolkien began working on *The Lord of the Rings* that he fully came to realize the importance of exact (albeit invented) maps for the creation of credible contexts.[31]

In spite of the exactness of the maps, the story not only filled the frames of the preceding geographical representations, but sometimes it ended up interrogating their accuracy and relevance. This is the case of Tom Bombadil's cabin in the Old Forest. Christopher Tolkien tells us (Tolkien, *Return of the Shadow* 114, 327–328) that his father did not seem to be very sure of the exact location of Tom's cabin—at least, the different drafts offer contradictory descriptions, the cabin being situated sometimes on the south side of the Withywindle, sometimes on the north. As it turned out, however, all these ponderings actually became quite redundant, because the final outcome shows a very blurred and vague sense of the geography surrounding the cabin, perhaps due to the mythic quality of the setting in the final version.[32] From the word, in this

---

31   Evidence for this may be found in another letter: "I wisely started with a map, and made the story fit (generally with meticulous care for distances). The other way about lands one in confusions and impossibilities, and in any case it is weary work to compose a map from a story—as I fear you have found" (*Letters* 177).

32   For a full discussion of the presence of mythic narrative paradigms in this episode, see Simonson ("Out of This World"). We may add that Tolkien, in one of his letters, claims that "We are not in 'fairy-land', but in real river-lands in autumn",

case the name Tom Bombadil, contexts arise and are geographically laid out by maps. The maps are then filled by stories that sometimes transcend the map-reality and take the shape of myth, which in turn affects the portrayal of space retroactively.

The digression of the Old Forest and the Barrow-downs is thus highly revealing of Tolkien's creative process, but it may also tell us something important about the author's general aims with the tale. According to novelistic standards of economy in plot-making, the adventure is actually quite superfluous, not adding anything of substance to the furthering of the story. One explanation for this may be that in Tolkien's narrative, the construction of a tight plot is not of *prime* importance. I have elsewhere argued (Simonson 2008) that this may be due to the fact that, apart from the novel, the narrative is heavily indebted to other narrative paradigms, such as romance and myth, in which plot is not always central. Shippey, on his part, claims that in *The Lord of the Rings*, "landscape and the beings attached to it are in a way the heroes", and that the digressive episodes in the story exist due to Tolkien's wish to connect the imagined world with our own, because

> they suggest very strongly a world which is more than imagined, whose supernatural qualities are close to entirely natural ones, one which has moreover been 'worn down', like ours, by time and by the process of lands and languages and people all growing up together over millenia. (109)[33]

Brian Rosebury takes the argument one step further and contends that in the Tom Bombadil-episode, "what looks like excess from the point of view of a plot-based structure is wholly necessary for a different kind of structure", alluding to the author's desire to create a feeling of intense

---

though it should be noted that the next sentence continues: "Goldberry *represents* the actual seasonal changes in such lands" (*Letters* 272, my italics). The insistence that the land is 'real' may of course also be due to the fact that Tolkien, in this letter, was criticising Forrest J. Ackerman's script for a projected screenplay based on *The Lord of the Rings*, in which he perceives a linguistic treatment leaning too far toward a childish fairy tale, and therefore feels the need to emphasise the "reality" of Middle-earth.

33   This description, while fitting for the portrayal of Ithilien, for instance, is not really valid for the Old Forest, which has not been deteriorated by time, languages and people—in fact, like Lórien, it is a place which to some extent exists *outside* time.

sympathy for Middle-earth itself (by extensive and careful portrayal) in order to make the reader care sufficiently about its potential destruction (32).

While I agree with Rosebury on this, I believe that the interpretation may be invested with further significance if we connect Tolkien's strategy with his particular creative impulse. If we believe Tolkien when he says that his story-telling creativity is based on discovering feasible contexts for his invented languages, the narrative as such necessarily becomes an exploration of Middle-earth itself, as if the writer were filling empty spaces on a rudimentary map as the writing progressed (which is basically the procedure outlined by the four volumes of *The History of The Lord of the Rings*). In short, if the exploration of context—that is, physical, cultural, and historical space—*as such* is a central part of *The Lord of the Rings*, the development of the plot is if not secondary then at least only of equal importance to the presentation of the discoveries. The fact that the Tom Bombadil-episode survived the subsequent revisions, in spite of its apparent redundancy within the framework of the larger narrative, indicates that for Tolkien, the discovery and revelation of the world had become just as important as the advancement of the plot.

We may venture to conclude that the idea of Recovery is at the heart of such an approach to story-telling, mainly because of the fact that the process engenders a simultaneous portrayal of different worlds. When the hobbits enter the Old Forest and arrive at Tom Bombadil's house and the Barrow-downs they break through to the world of myth, and when we return to the familiar world of Bree, we know that it only exists on a simultaneous level. Which is more real, Bree or the Barrow-downs? No answer is given, because the text provides us with three different realities of equal importance. The invented (though coherent) map-reality of Middle-earth and the mythic, "super-supernatural" realm (which transcends the map-reality) in which Tom Bombadil and the Barrow-wights dwell, simultaneously co-exist and convey a sense of Recovery by revealing ancient elements (which used to be hidden by a routine perception) in the reader's contemporary reality, in turn alluded to by the literary, cultural, religious and historical correspondences between the phenomena of Middle-earth and those of our own world.

As the hobbits move on, Tolkien keeps putting the reader in contact with societies defined by the languages they speak, different from our own but at the same time similar, that transmit an elusive scent of our own past and cultural heritage. To be able to grasp the essence of these societies, we must necessarily contemplate the reality designated by their words with different eyes (in other words, we must recover an earlier vision of our place in the world), but this does not imply that we need to lose touch with the present. In *The Lord of the Rings*, the word, and the secondary world that takes shape around it, is key to the myth-making and to a deeper understanding of our place in the modern world.

Words may be evidence of man's fall, Tolkien implies, but at the same time they present us with the unique possibility to make use of the subcreative gift which, if efficiently expressed, may open up paths towards a new unity with both the natural and the supernatural worlds. Tolkien shared this conviction with the Romantics and the Transcendentalists. However, by using a four-fold process, from word-making to myth-making by way of map-making and a very special kind of plot-making, largely aimed at presenting his discoveries, Tolkien takes the previous ideas of Recovery and sub-creation one step further. Hence, while the expression may be rooted in the same concerns, the spontaneous and intuitive use of language hailed by Emerson as the proper means to put us back in touch with Oneness, is somewhat differently handled by Tolkien. For Tolkien, Art is a gift—in this context a capacity to explore and reveal what "the drab blur of triteness and familiarity" has hidden from us, by means of creating imaginary though plausible contexts for the half-familiar words he invented. This gift, at once linguistic and imaginative, is what defines the particularity of Tolkien's approach to Recovery within the framework of Neoplatonic, Romantic and Transcendentalist thinking, filtered through the Edwardian literary mode of fantasy.

When Ursula Le Guin enters the literary scene with her *Earthsea* books, she thus takes part in a tradition of fantasy and nature writing which was Romantic in origin, partly American in its transcendental approach to nature, Edwardian in inspiration and Tolkienian in execution—but also heavily informed by the idiosyncrasies of the American West where she grew up as a person and came to her own as a writer. The rest of this book aims to analyse Le Guin's portrayal of nature against this imaginative, cultural and literary background, but since the shadow of Tolkien looms so large over almost all subsequent epic fantasy, we need to take one last look at what it was Le Guin departed from in her fantastic renderings of the West before we embark on a detailed analysis of Earthsea.

The portrayal of the West in Tolkien's works

It is only natural that J.R.R. Tolkien's deep knowledge of the languages, literature, history and culture of the European North and North-west should provide him with subject matter for his own literary works. As a consequence, many of these works obliquely reflect the long and rich history of myth, literature and developing languages that had collectively shaped the culture of the British Isles over many centuries. Focusing, as he did, on Europe, he hardly incorporated any reference whatsoever to the American West in his writings. Instead, the general idea about the West that comes through in Tolkien's works is that of a legendary realm beyond the sea, an enchanted and blessed paradise—shaped along the lines of various pre-existing medieval and classical notions, which he synthesised in fictional guise for the genre he was so instrumental in creating.

One of the works that inspired Tolkien the most, the Old English epic *Beowulf*, provided him with a suggestive hint of what the Scandinavians of the period believed to lie beyond the sea in the West. In this work it is told of how Scyld Sceafing, the legendary founder of the Danish kingdom, arrives in a boat from the West as a child, and is committed to the same sea in a funerary ship after his death. Tolkien, in his comments on *Beowulf*, says that "He came out of the Unknown beyond the Great Sea, and returned into It" (Tolkien, *Beowulf* 151), implying that this is proof of some "actual belief in a magical land or otherworld located 'over the sea'" (Tolkien, *Beowulf* 152). In *The Silmarillion*, Tolkien firmly placed the immortal realm of the gods, Valinor, in the West across the sea from Middle-earth, which is the dwelling of mortal men. In doing so, he also reflects the Celtic traditions of voyages to the western lands of bliss and wonder:

After a westward sea voyage across the sea from Anglo-Saxon England, Eriol, the narrator of *The Book of Lost Tales*, arrives at an island called the Lonely Isle, where he meets and befriends the Elves, who tell him of their legends. The parallels with Snorri Sturluson's *Prose Edda* are obvious: just as the Lonely Isle is situated next to Valinor, in the Icelandic work Alfheim ("Elfhome") is located in the divine Asgard.

By and large, Tolkien's literary rendering of the West is a suggestive mélange of various traditions featuring a divine or supernatural region beyond the sea, whether it be Celtic or Norse. Garth aptly summarises the combined heritage in the following way:

After leaving ordinary waters, a mariner sailing Tolkien's Great Sea would encounter first the Magic or Enchanted Isles … Beyond [these], the Shadowy Seas form a final barrier. They recall the region "shrouded in darkness or mist" in the vicinity of Vinland, described by eleventh-century chronicler Adam of Bremen; or the obscuring fog through which St Brendan voyages to reach the Land of Happiness in the ninth-century Irish *Navigatio*. (*The Worlds of J.R.R. Tolkien*, 66)

In Tolkien's legendarium, the idea of an earthly paradise in the West is enhanced by the island of Númenor, akin to the Biblical Promised Land. Here, the descendants of the Men who helped the Elves in the wars against Morgoth are given an opportunity for a fresh start on a Western island, whose benign climate and fertile soil ensure a blissful existence for the wise and skillful Númenóreans, who enjoy extremely long lives and are given great creative powers. However, the evil semi-god Sauron corrupts the mortal Númenóreans and make them break their promise to the gods, urging them instead to conquer the divine Blessed Realm of Valinor. As a punishment for this transgression, Númenor is destroyed and the immortal lands of Valinor are transferred beyond "the circles of the world", to a place which only the Elves can access.

IV Nature, Fantasy and the American West in Ursula K. Le Guin's *Earthsea*

Ursula K. Le Guin was born in Berkeley in 1929 and settled in Portland, Oregon, in 1959 after ten years in Europe and on the East Coast. The West thus framed her experiences abroad, and gave shape to much of her writing. Kunzru, writing on Le Guin's status as a Western American writer, holds that the "coastal tradition looks west to the Pacific, with a wilderness at its back and European or East coast cities very far away", and quotes Le Guin as saying that she felt "'very uppity' about the 'parochialism and snobbishness' of the East Coast literary establishment. 'The idea that everybody lives in a large city in the east, it's such a strange thing for an American to think'". Kunzru implies that wild nature and the immensity of the Pacific gave shape to Le Guin's imaginary worlds.

Le Guin, growing up in California and developing as a writer in Oregon, was naturally exposed to many of the core characteristics of the American West. Both California and Oregon are bordered by the vast Pacific Ocean, and in one very strong and tangible sense, the coastline was equated with the end of a long journey of western expansion. In another sense, however, it was the beginning of an imaginative journey that gave shape to the previous experience. To get to the West Coast, several generations of pioneers had progressively made their way across the continent, conquering nature as they went. As they did so, the white people displaced the original Native Americans and Chicanos who were there before them, justifying their conquests with a mythical notion that the West was their "Promised Land", and it was their "Manifest Destiny" to settle there. I have capitalized these two concepts because of their powerful hold on the popular imagination of the settlers, to which was added idea of the frontier, ever moving towards the Pacific in the Far West.

These conceptual notions were reinforced by the so-called "Turner thesis", as outlined by the historian Frederick Jackson Turner in his 1894 essay *The Significance of the Frontier in American History*. Briefly put, Turner holds that the frontier—and especially the idea of a people pushing the frontier westwards—was instrumental in giving shape to American democracy. Not only did it help celebrate certain notions of freedom and equality, it also consolidated a culture of violence and brewed a contempt for what was perceived as the high-brow intellectualism of the East Coast, and for outdated European cultural manifestations and attitudes (Regenbogen 70).

In spite of this, the European heritage of most pioneers inevitably informed the popular myth of the West, and white Anglo-Saxon protestants became the dominating elite also here, imposing their own world-view and political and economic structures without taking into much consideration—or even blatantly eradicated—the cultural roots, rights and needs of the people that were living there before their arrival. The fascination and fear engendered by these native peoples are reflected in North American literature of the period, in which the natives occupied a place that in European literature was reserved for mythological beings (Rexroth 35). As the new myth of the West was taking shape, the pre-existing myths were transformed, and the particular conditions of the frontier also intervened decisively to modify the stories and the character of the white heroes in their encounters with nineteenth-century versions of the noble savage, which ended up establishing the parameters for a particularly Western American hero (Simonson and Gilete 56).

Meanwhile, the real natives were killed, displaced or carried off to reservations, and rapidly acquired an iconic status, a little like the Western American nature itself, which was celebrated for its monumental beauty, but also destroyed by intensive farming and overpopulation. Together with the vastness of the natural expanses, the native population of Western America turned into something old, quaint and picturesque in the popular imagination, a paradox and a tangible contrast with the rapid urban expansion of the white settlements.

Le Guin's imaginative transformation of the West

Thus, the natural reality of both California and Oregon, where Le Guin spent most of her life, was not only a defining feature of life in this region, it also acted as a catalyst of mythical notions of the West as a Promised Land and Manifest Destiny, which could be accessed through a moving Frontier. The idea of the West as a natural space imbued and informed by mythical and cultural narratives obviously held powerful imaginative possibilities for a writer like Le Guin, who in her youth became obsessed with the recently emerged genres of fantasy and science fiction. Just like the Celts and the Vikings, living on the fringes of the vast Atlantic, had imagined all sorts of insular wonders in the West, as a child growing up in Berkeley Le Guin's mind would stray towards another ocean, the even vaster Pacific. For example, the Farallon islands, off the coast of San Francisco, stimulated Le Guin's imagination, and in her mind, they turned into a fantastic representation of

> the loneliest place, the farthest west you could go . . . And they have such a beautiful name. *Los farallones* means cliffs, crags; a lovely word, and in English it gathers echoes—far away and all alone. . . But that's all I know about the Farallones, where I will never go (Le Guin, *The Wave in the Mind* 24).

The imaginative reality of the West inspired both wonder and awe in Le Guin, but the myth of the American West was also a troubling cultural feature of the region. As a child she visited Indian Reservations with her parents, the famous anthropologists Alfred and Theodora Kroeber, who had come from the East Coast to study the Native Americans in Northern California, seeing in California examples of ancient cultures in the process of being destroyed or transformed. In this way, from an early age Le Guin became deeply sensitive to the fact that there were other realities in the West, and other judgments to be made, apart from the narratives tailored to suit the needs of the dominating social class.

Whether or not it was a conscious reaction to such experiences, already as a child Le Guin took a keen interest in whatever was not mainstream. In literature, this translated into a predilection for fantasy and science fiction. Clearly, when Le Guin builds her Earthsea drama, which reaches its climax in the Far West, her narrative descends from

European high fantasy, as established mainly by Tolkien, but which was also based on historical narrative traditions such as the epic, medieval romance and the Gothic novel, as we have seen. However, when applying the Western American imaginative reality and her own life experiences to the genre, Le Guin ends up depicting a world which, among other things, calls into question the white ethnical hegemony and its urban-centred societies. In terms of her portrayal of nature, which is our main concern in this book, Le Guin's vision of the natural world of Earthsea is heavily informed by Eastern thinking. Mid-century California witnessed a growing interest in Eastern spirituality, and the Romantic (or Transcendentalist) urge to return to nature was also particularly strong in the Bay Area. In Earthsea, the yang-ying conceptualization of Taoist philosophy readily comes through in the lines from the genesis myth of the invented world, *The Creation of Éa*, which is quoted on the first page of the original trilogy in order to set the scene for the kind of reality which will be described in the books:

> Only in silence the word,
> only in dark the light,
> only in dying life:
> bright the hawk's flight
> on the empty sky.
> (*A Wizard of Earthsea*)

One of the central tenets of Taoism is the need to respect the environment. In Cooper's words, the Taoist view is that "Once [man] has become divorced from nature and has lost the sense of communion with all things, the Oneness, he starts on the downward path which leads to destruction, not only of nature but of his own spiritual life, for the two are intimately associated; as he kills nature, so he kills himself" (Cooper 66). This stance is reflected by the "fallen" mage Cob's voluntary displacement from the natural world in Earthsea, which leads not only to his own destruction, but also to that of the global environment. Throughout the books of Earthsea, environmental concerns arise as a consequence of treating nature and its myriad of life-forms as something fundamentally different from humans.

One leitmotif in the books (as in the Myth of the American West) is the idea of a Blessed Realm situated in the Far West. In Le Guin's world, this is where the dragons used to live—creatures who have become estranged and differentiated from humans, and powerful guardians of the magical Old Speech. However, a transgression once occurred in this place: human mages attempted to gain immortality, stealing the land "west of west" from the dragons to create a paradise for themselves in which they would not be bound to the natural cycles but could lead immortal lives. The mages then erected a wall between this supposedly blessed place and its surroundings, but the Paradise has since dried up. Nothing now changes, and the immortal souls are trapped, leading a dreary existence. At the bottom of the valley of the dead is a dry river, and beyond that, the Mountains of Pain, which can be crossed to return to life.

This territory, the so-called "Dry Land", is entered by Ged and the future king Lebannen in *The Farthest Shore*, the third part of the original trilogy. Again, scenery from the American West may have served as an inspiration for Le Guin here: the lugubrious setting obviously recalls California's own Death Valley, bordered by barren mountains and emblematic of the persistent droughts that have affected a region which was not naturally equipped for hosting a booming population, or for sustaining extensive farming, and thus suffers the devastating consequences of erosion. It is also a land that has been stolen from its original inhabitants. In *The Other Wind*, Le Guin tells of how the Wall of the Dry Land is finally destroyed, freeing the trapped souls to rejoin the cycle of death and rebirth. This is an implicitly Taoist critique of the Myth of the West, the ultimately Christian notion of a Promised Land and a Manifest Destiny, that gave rise to a relentless pursuit of an earthly paradise, and to an obsessive and possessive view of the land, which in turn caused great suffering for the minorities originally dwelling there, and put a great strain on the natural world.

Le Guin's vision of the Dry Land, the Wall, and the Dragons in the West thus becomes an imaginative echo and a rebuttal of the American obsession with westward expansion in search of the Promised Land, pictured as an earthly paradise. California used to be that promised land—and just like the Far West in Earthsea used to be the mythical realm of the dragons, the Far West in medieval European traditions and in Tolkien's works also held the promise of divine bliss and bounty. Once the West is colonized and urbanized, however, the Promised Land becomes disenchanted—in reality as well as in Le Guin's imaginative accounts of the process. As Tolkien once wrote, "The unfortunate existence of America on the other side of a strictly limited Atlantic Ocean is most constantly and vividly present in the imagination ... there are no magic islands in our Western sea" (Tolkien, *The Story of Kullervo* 113–114). In Earthsea, a wall is erected around the site of conquest, and the dragons are driven away. The immortal souls become trapped, and the very environment that was supposed to sustain everlasting happiness dries up, bringing death in life and perpetual suffering. A parallel is found in Tolkien's earthly paradise of Númenor, which in the end was not enough for the mortal men who dwelled there and wished to be immortal, thus bringing about their own ruin.

However, in Le Guin's works the eternal is not beyond the world in the same sense that Tolkien's Valinor is; eternity is *in* the world and imbued with Taoist beliefs rather than Christian or Classical myth. As opposed to Tolkien's world-vision, where both Men and Elves have to leave the world (albeit in different directions), Earthsea is based on the principle of rebirth. The Earthsea books thus exhibit a transition from Tolkien's fantasy-tradition based on medieval and classical sources with Christian undertones, to a kind of fantasy grounded in the real American West of the second half of the twentieth century, with Taoist overtones—reflecting contemporary issues such as anti-imperialism, issues of race and gender, and environmentalism.

The world of Earthsea: Precedents

Dragons, having been present since the very beginnings of Earthsea, hold a role of considerable importance regarding the shaping and development of this world and its inhabitants. The following section aims to show how Le Guin portrayed the dragons of *Earthsea*[34], imbuing them

---

34 Although the novels of *The Earthsea Cycle* will be referred to individually, all of them, with the exception of *The Other Wind*, are included in the omnibus edition entitled *Earthsea: the First Four Books* and the collection *Tales From Earthsea*.

with a symbolism that renders them representatives of nature. In addition, we will refer to a key event that these creatures are involved in, which will result in a complete reshaping of humanity's attitude towards nature.

In order to fully grasp the relevance of the dragons in Le Guin's saga, it is essential that we look at how they are represented. Warren G. Rochelle argues that, due to the clear connections between Earthsea and "the medieval world of the West" ("The Emersonian Choice: Connections Between Dragons and Humans in Le Guin's *Earthsea* Cycle" 420), it seems inevitable that the dragons dwelling in this fictional world are also "associated with all four of the ancient medieval elements: earth, fire, water and air" ("The Emersonian Choice" 420). Nevertheless, as readers move through the several novels that comprise this series, an idea about still-greater implications surrounding dragons inevitably arises. In fact, Le Guin herself claimed that "these are dragons of a new world, America, and the visionary forms of an old woman's mind" (*Earthsea Revisioned* 22), hinting that the connotations of Earthsea's dragons go beyond those of the more classical medieval ones[35]. This symbolism is related to the aforementioned elements of nature that Rochelle points out as characterising Le Guin's dragons, since it could be argued that these are representatives of "Nature, in its raw, untamed beauty" (Rochelle, "The Emersonian Choice" 423). Even Le Guin herself seems to support this claim when she mentions that these creatures principally showcase the idea of "wildness. What is not owned" (*Earthsea Revisioned* 22). It is to this very perception that we hold, namely, to the idea that dragons are direct representatives of nature in the world of Earthsea. The implications of this would be that Le Guin is here proposing a paradigmatic change concerning dragons, ridding them of their classical Christian connotations as purely evil and dangerous to humankind, originally linked to the serpent of Eden (Ansgar Kelly 304), which persisted through the Middle Ages (Hodges 110). Le Guin, by contrast, portrays them as an essential part of nature, placing humanity, instead, as a hazardous and destabilising element, as will be shown below. Hereby, the following lines will be devoted to exploring these issues, drawing evidence from the texts

---

35   We should call to mind medieval Anglo-Saxon antecedents such as the dragon appearing in *Beowulf*, and the biblical legend of Saint George and the dragon.

that comprise Le Guin's saga, in order to make clearer the potential connection between dragons and nature and the consequence of this on the attitude of humans towards their environment.

To start with, we should draw attention to the type of relationship that dragons appear to have with the world in which they live. In Le Guin's *A Description of Earthsea* is written that "songs and stories indicate that dragons existed before any other living creature" (380). It should here be remarked that the oldest representative of their race is called Kalessin, described as "of great age, of years beyond remembering" (Le Guin, *The Farthest Shore* 627). In addition, it is worth pointing to the role that dragons presumably played in Earthsea's creation, hinted at in the following lines: "it may be that Segoy is a name for the Earth itself. Some think all dragons, or certain dragons, or certain people are manifestations of Segoy" (Le Guin, *Description* 391). The identity of Segoy is not made clear, the only thing that we know about it being its role as god-creator of the world of Earthsea. However, it is certainly significant that Kalessin, the head and eldest of the race of dragons, is addressed by Tehanu, a character who is half-human and half-dragon, as Segoy (Le Guin, *Tehanu* 886).

Related to the idea of the paragraph above, the apparent link between the dragons and the so-called Language of the Making is another feature that can be useful to highlight their closeness to nature. About this language, also known as True Speech, we know that it was the language "with which Segoy created the islands of Earthsea at the beginning of time, [and] is presumably an infinite language, as it names all things" (Le Guin, *Description* 383). Thanks to the fact that this language contains the true names of everything—people, animals, the elements, etc.—its users are granted absolute power over that which they name. Interestingly, and for reasons that will be shown below, this is the native tongue of the dragons and only dragons, implying that no human being will ever be "a true speaker of it" (Le Guin, *Tehanu* 856). Indeed, the dragons' bond with this language goes far beyond them being mere users of it, as we learn that "the dragon and the speech of the dragon are one. One being" (Le Guin, *Tehanu* 856) and that "they do not learn [it]. ... They are" (Le Guin, *Tehanu* 856). Such is their knowledge and command of the True Speech, that they can manipulate it to serve their own purposes, so that unlike men, whose "use ... binds [them] to truth" (Le Guin, *A*

Wizard of Earthsea 109), dragons "can lie in it, twisting the true words to false ends, catching the unwary hearer in a maze of mirror-words each of which reflects the truth and none of which leads anywhere" (Le Guin, *A Wizard of Earthsea* 109).

Contrasted to dragons are humans, who, in order to gain knowledge and mastery of this language, have to learn it. Among them, those who learn the most words are the wizards, who later on use it to make magic (Le Guin, *Description* 383). Those who gain the deepest knowledge of True Speech are considered Dragonlords, "one whom the dragons will speak with" (Le Guin, *The Tombs of Atuan* 323). Thanks to their knowledge of the Language of the Making, they have great power, and the greatest and last of them is Archmage Sparrowhawk. We learn that Sparrowhawk's power is far greater than that of his peers, as he is able to continue casting and keeping his spells even when others' power has waned considerably (Le Guin, *AWoE* 208–209), and to control even the most destructive forces of nature (Le Guin, *TToA* 346). Having said that, his power is, of course, not limitless (Le Guin, *TtoA* 365). We are thus able to detect the close link between this language and nature, the former being a source of life and a gateway to the possession and use of nature's powers, among other things. The fact that this language constitutes a vital part of the dragons' being enhances their relationship with nature.

Another interesting feature that hints at a relationship between nature and dragons is the superior position that they occupy in relation to men. Actually, the former regard the latter as somehow irrelevant, as they seldom meddle in their business. About this, for instance, Sparrowhawk mentions that "dragons think [humans] are amusing" (Le Guin, *TToA* 353). Going back to the figure of Kalessin, we find more instances of this hierarchy, as when it is said that, for this dragon men "are like mayflies" (Le Guin, *TFS* 579). One final example of dragons' superiority to men can be found in a scene described in Le Guin's *The Farthest Shore* (1972), which runs as follows:

> Never in the memory of man, scarcely in the memory of legend, had any dragon braved the walls visible and invisible of the well-defended isle. Yet this one did not hesitate, but flew on ponderous wings and heavily over the western shore of Roke, and above the villages and fields, to the green hill that rises over Thwil town. There at last it stooped softly to the earth, and raised its red wings and folded them, and crouched on the summit of Roke Knoll. (631)

In this scene, Kalessin is bringing a seriously hurt Sparrowhawk to the isle of Roke, which is defended by magic against anyone who tries to enter it without the consent of its rulers. However, Kalessin, being beyond wizard—that is, human—power, can enter at will. We can here see how the superiority of dragons over men may be based on their greater power. Indeed, dragons seem to be extremely powerful, and Kalessin is described as a being of "brute strength and size" (Le Guin, *TFS* 628) within whom "life burned in fire" (Le Guin, *TFS* 629).

Next, we may mention the psychological consequences that an encounter with, or the mere presence of dragons implies for a human being. One of these encounters features Kalessin and Tenar, a woman who becomes a key character in the development of the *Earthsea* saga. The meeting hints at a type of well-being felt by just pronouncing the name of the eldest of dragons: "[Tenar] looked out into the vast levels of air and cloud and said in her mind, once, *Kalessin*. And her mind cleared, as that air was clear" (Le Guin, *Tehanu* 777). The second encounter worth mentioning involves Sparrowhawk, on a voyage to the westernmost isles of Earthsea, also known as the Dragon's Run, where only dragons live, and "no man living … had sailed … or seen it, except the Archmage" (Le Guin, *TFS* 577). The witnessing of the flight of dragons on those remote isles must have marked Sparrowhawk deeply, since years later, recalling that moment, he expresses that "though I came to forget or regret all I have ever done, yet I would remember that once I saw the dragons aloft on the wind at sunset above the western isles; and I would be content" (Le Guin, *TFS* 442).

A final remark on the topic of dragons and nature concerns the way in which dragons are portrayed as good or evil, for which purpose the following quotation will be illuminating:

> Kalessin said to [the dragons], 'You let evil turn you into evil. You have been mad. You are sane again, but so long as the winds blow from the east you can never be what you were, free of both good and evil' (Le Guin, *The Other Wind* 151).

Dragons had originally been neither good nor bad, which David Naimon, in a collection of interviews he conducted with Le Guin called *Ursula K. Le Guin: Conversations on Writing with David Naimon* (2018), attributes to the fact that the world of Earthsea "is not a Manichean world, one where darkness and light are in opposition" (55). Indeed, it was the winds coming from the east, that is, where humans live, that turned them evil. As Warren Rochelle remarks, this happened because "the mages kept the knowledge of the Old Speech that let them manipulate Nature–and in doing so, eventually brought evil to creatures that were neither good nor evil; they just were" ("The Emersonian Choice" 425). Nevertheless, we should bear in mind that during the period in which the stories of the *Earthsea* saga take place, the dragon race displays features of both good and evil, in that some of its individuals will engage with humans in a hostile manner, while others will seek to work together with them.

To conclude, then, which are the features that make Earthsea's dragons into representatives of nature? First, we have seen that dragons were the first beings to have ever dwelt in this world, and they are repeatedly related to Earthsea's originating force and figure, Segoy. This reminds us of the role of the forces of nature on our own planet, forming the origins of our dwellings, and the source of all life that has come after. Similarly, we have talked about the dragons' communion with the Language of the Making, that is, the primary source of creation. Considering the power that it grants its speaker, True Speech may be thought of as a sort of guide to the principles and functioning of the world; a passage through which to gain knowledge and possession of its hidden powers. Its innate relation to dragons increases the symbolism of them as nature. The fact that human beings need to learn this language and the resulting study, magic, and power drawn from it, may indicate our own science (Le Guin, "Entretien avec Ursula K. Le Guin" 146), always looking at new ways to unfold the secrets of nature and learn more about its ways.

We should also consider the hierarchy determining the relation between dragons and humans, the former being always above the latter due to their greater power, the same way as nature is above us. No matter how far we may think our control over the ecosystem reaches, nature showcases its hidden power once and again, thus, in a way, resetting the hierarchy and making us aware of its greatness. We also mentioned nature's positive effects upon humans. Even in our world, we constantly resort to nature and the environment in order to seek that internal, psychological welfare. as if the sight of and contact with it could make us forget all about our mundane concerns and make us simply rejoice in what we see.

The last idea that has been pointed out as a connection between dragons and nature is how, until humans arrived and classified dragons according to their own beliefs, they were above the parameters of good and evil. Similarly, we could say that the same thing happens in our relationship with nature. Humans tend to deem nature good if, for instance, the seasons are fair and the crops grow abundant; it is evil, if, on the contrary, natural disasters happen that result in heavy human casualties. We tend to forget that nature stands well above those Manichean classifications: that nature just is. Here, Le Guin portraying her dragons as capable of creating and destroying may refer to nature being at once a source of life and an extremely destructive power. Such an incorporative representation of dragons and, ultimately, the natural world, exactly mirrors Le Guin's own environmental experience in the West. California, Le Guin's home estate, includes untameable wilderness, hostile and barren landscapes, and huge distances (Simonson & Montero Gilete 29). Apart from this, it is also a place of contrasts. According to Andrew Rolle,

> it offers man virtually every physical, climatic, geologic, and vegetational combination: the wettest weather and the driest; poor sandy soil in the south-eastern desert regions and rich loam in the great Central Valley; some of the hottest recorded temperatures on earth and also the coldest; the highest mountain in the United States outside Alaska . . . and the lowest point in the country. (4)

Nevertheless, we should not mistake diversity and contrast for tranquillity, but should bear in mind this estate's high seismic incidence (Rawls & Bean 3). All this implies that California's environment is far from being "superficial" (Le Guin, "Review of *Benediction*" 230), largely owing to its "impassively dangerous and beautiful landscape" (Le Guin, "Review of *Ledoyt*" 225).

Having explained the features that may lead us to consider the dragons in Earthsea as direct symbols of nature, we now move on to a key event in the history of this world, which shaped it for ever and in which dragons played a crucial role. Before doing so, however, we should briefly explain how the world of Earthsea came into being and who its first inhabitants were. As stated above, the almighty god Segoy spoke the Language of the Making, and thus "raised the islands of the world from the sea in the beginning of time" (Le Guin, *Tehanu* 650). We learn that the first inhabitants of this newly created world were a race composed of both dragons and humans, who had an innate knowledge of True Speech, the same language spoken by Segoy. However, this original race very soon branched out into other individual and distinct races, in an event known as the Vedurnan. One of these branches was formed by those individuals who

> became more and more in love with flight wildness, and would have less and less to do with the works of making, or with study and learning, [seeking] only to fly and fly farther and farther, ... seeking more freedom and more (Le Guin, *Tehanu* 650).

These are the ones who would gradually become dragons as we imagine them today, and who kept their knowledge of True Speech.

Contrasted to these are those who would ultimately become humans. About them, it is said that they

> came to care little for flight, but gathered up treasure, wealth, things made, things learned. They built houses, strongholds to keep their treasures in, so they could pass all they gained to their children, ever seeking more increase and more (Le Guin, *Tehanu* 650).

It should also be noted that humans lost their knowledge of True Speech after a while. In a sense, what we can see in this division is that one of the main differences between these new races of dragons and humans is that, while the former chooses to merely be, the latter chooses making and possessing, as testified in this verse:

> Men chose the yoke
> dragons the wing.
> Men to own,
> dragons no thing. (Le Guin, *Description* 400)

After this division, the relationship between dragons and humans turned into one of enmity, in which the races attacked each other for survival. This hostility resulted in a geographical separation: while dragons went to live in the western winds of Earthsea, humans—steadily increasing in number—started to build their cities in the eastern part of the world (Le Guin, *Tehanu* 651). Vedurnan also resulted in the creation of an additional, third, breed, formed of individuals who would remain somewhere in between dragons and humans, acknowledging the existing kinship between the two races, and who

> still both human and dragon, still winged, went not east but west, on over the Open
> Sea, till they came to the other side of the world[, where] they live in peace, great
> winged beings both wild and wise, with human mind and dragon heart (Le Guin,
> *Tehanu* 651).

Thus, certain individuals are still born as both dragon and human, who, in a sense, know of their kinship with the other race.

We may think that all of this could be hinting at a possible alienation between humanity and the natural world. Indeed, we can find certain characteristics of such an estrangement throughout the different human societies of Earthsea. First, we must recall what happened to the race of humans when they became separated from the dragons, namely, that, among other things, they decided to forsake their knowledge of True Speech. This was a language deeply rooted in nature, since it was used in the making of this world. As a result of humans thus neglecting its wisdom, their new languages would also come to reflect such a loss. For instance, Hardic, the predominant language in Earthsea, is said to have its roots in Old Speech, although, now, "it has no more power in it than any other tongue of men" (Le Guin, *AWoE* 27). Such is also the case in the Kargad Lands, were the local language, Kargish, has similarly strayed from this original source language, and we learn that magic is very rare there, since the making of magic needs the Language of the Making.

As a whole—and perhaps as a result of this loss of True Speech—Earthsea's human society has entered a phase of social and political progress, a consequence of which is further alienation from nature. An example of this is that, by the end of the saga, the dragons have disappeared from the archipelago (Le Guin, *TOW* 246). Similarly, Sparrowhawk is Earthsea's last ever Archmage—the last individual with a deep knowledge of the Language of the Making—and after him will follow a lineage of kings with no training in the art of magic (Le Guin, *Tehanu* 798). These tendencies are examples of how "the balance changes" (Le Guin, *TOW* 152), indicating that the world is undergoing a paradigm shift. More precise and particular examples of this shift can be found, for instance, on the island of Atuan. In the past, Atuan's inhabitants worshipped the darkest and most destructive powers of the earth—referred to as Nameless Ones—and then, in more recent times, turned their worship to human-like god figures (Le Guin, *TToA* 252). On the isle of Havnor, we find another instance of natural worship being forsaken, as in a place called Aurun, also known as the Lips of Paor. This is "a great crack in the ground, a black gap twenty feet wide or more" (Le Guin, *TOW* 170). What is peculiar about this place is that here dwell the so-called Old Powers of the earth, "the chthonic or gaean forces manifest as forces of place" (Le Guin, *Description* 413), akin to the forces worshipped in Atuan. However, with the passing of time, the locals have forgotten the knowledge of the power of this place, and now use it as a place to dispose of their waste, thus defiling it (Le Guin, *TOW* 171). Nevertheless, across the different lands of Earthsea, communities that maintain a tighter connection with nature still exist. We find instances of these in the Kargad Lands, who have continued with a clandestine adoration of the Old Powers; and the Children of the Open Sea, a community living in floating cities composed of several tied rafts who acquire their basic supplies from what the sea has to offer them, such as fish and seaweed (Le Guin, *TFS* 541).

All in all, however, we have seen how the aforementioned change is predominant in Earthsea's human societies, gradually driving them away from nature. An implication of this attitude is a dramatic change in the relationship between humanity and its ecosystem. We could say that, at the beginning of time, humans and nature engaged in a horizontal manner, meaning that theirs was an association between equals, where both stood on the same level. The division and estrangement derived from the Vedurnan converted this relationship into a vertical one, where each side struggled for the upper hand, and thus gain power and control over the other. This hostile mindset, particularly of humans claiming their rank above nature, is present in places like Pendor and Havnor. Regarding the former, we are told that the lords of that rich city were "[sending] their sons west dragon hunting. In sport" (Le Guin, *The Finder* 70). As for the latter, some people of that island are said to have engaged with the environment in utterly destructive ways for the sake of obtaining profit from a mineral mined from the earth (Le Guin, *The Finder* 47).

We find the last example of this vertical relationship in an event that took place soon after the races of humans and dragons were divided as a consequence of the Vedurnan. This could be said to be the first instance of humanity claiming and achieving ownership over the lands of the dragons—that is, the natural environment—which they perceived to be a "realm ... not of the body only" (Le Guin, *TOW* 227), but rather a paradisiacal place. As Orm Irian, one belonging to the race in between dragons and humans, expresses it, "you wanted things to make and keep ... But you were not content with your share. You wanted not only your cares, but our freedom. You wanted the wind! And by the spells and wizardries of those oath-breakers, you stole half our realm from us, walled it away from life and light, so that you could live there forever" (Le Guin, *TOW* 227). In a sense, we here witness human colonialism in action, the victims, in this case being dragons, and thus, as we have seen, nature. As will be shown below, the aftermath of such an enterprise and attitude towards nature, one implying estrangement and, in some cases, hostility, will be disastrous and manifold for mankind.

Life in a Fallen World

Regarding the place that nature occupies in Le Guin's work, Tonia Payne suggests that, at first glance, this is not a central topic in her stories, indeed

> the relationship between humans and nature in her texts is usually subordinate to the story, a story that is 'about' something else entirely. She ... is telling stories in which the natural world is described as physical setting and in which human relationships with that world are a significant but usually subordinate theme (37).

However, the fact that Le Guin frequently introduces the topic of nature by way of human approaches to it, should not lead us to think that she is thus relegating nature to a peripheral position. Rather, nature is a fundamental pillar on which Le Guin's literature rests, triggering the "awareness of the need to confront human interactions with and ideas about nature" (Payne 37). In a similar manner, Scott Russel Sanders writes that Le Guin "[seeks] to understand our life as continuous with the life of nature; [projecting] 'the little human morality play' against the 'wilderness raging around'" (191).

We have already been able to see how an expansionist/colonialist activity on behalf of humans and their relationship with nature appear to be closely linked. Interestingly enough for our study, a nation's appropriation of lands has historically involved significant damage to nature.

As Jonathan Bate claims, "imperialism has always been accompanied by ecological exploitation" (100) and "environmental degradation" (76), a thought also shared by Greg Garrard (133).

A Natural Universe?

The crucial part played by dragons may also hint at an additional implication, which will be explored in the following paragraphs. What we would like to suggest is that, by proposing a universe that has been created by a figure—Segoy—showcasing such tight bonds with the forces of nature, Le Guin might be subverting the Judaeo-Christian paradigm of the society in which she was born and raised. What her work proposes, then, is a move from the anthropocentric myth of creation, as is the Judaeo-Christian, to an ecocentric one, as presented in Earthsea. Indeed, Le Guin deemed religion to be a foundational part of, among other things, culture and art ("Ursula K. Le Guin: Free Speech, Press Are 'Liberty in Action'", par. 9). Making use of her cultural heritage, she thus constructs a critique of it, offering up an alternative to its man-centred world view. As Lev Grossman said of Le Guin, she "is a writer who ... simply seized the patriarchal-Christian fantasy tradition laid down by Lewis and Tolkien by the scruff of its neck and reimagined it from a feminist, post-Judaeo-Christian point of view" ("An Interview with Ursula K. Le Guin" [*Time*], par. 2).

For a person of her strong feminist beliefs and attachment to the natural world, it is no wonder that the Christian tradition is seen as an ideology that, although necessary for the cultural development of Western society, has shaped humanity's mind in a not fully appropriate way, and for too long (John Loftus, qtd. in Mehta, par. 5). Certainly, man's historically central role and hegemony in Western civilisation can be traced back to the Christian conception of the genesis of our universe. Robert H. Ayers (155) and Lynn White Junior agree on the biblical origins of this idea of man's uncontested power. White Junior offers an explanation that is worth quoting at length:

God had created Adam and, as an afterthought, Eve to keep man from being lonely. Man named all the animals, thus establishing his dominance over them. God planned all of this explicitly for man's benefit and rule: no item in the physical creation had any purpose save to serve man's purposes. And, although man's body is made of clay, he is not simply part of nature: he is made in God's image.

Especially in its Western form, Christianity is the most anthropocentric religion the world has seen. As early as the second century both Tertulian and Saint Irenaeus of Lyons were insisting that when God shaped Adam he was foreshadowing the image of the incarnate Christ, the Second Adam. (9)

In light of this, our Western civilisation, which has followed Christianity as its spiritual guide for several centuries now, has also developed a social hierarchy in which man sits on top and rules every bit of our world. Le Guin was extremely critical of this, writing that

Civilized Man says: I am Self, I am Master, all the rest is Other—outside, below, underneath, subservient. I own, I use, I explore, I exploit, I control. What I do is what matters. What I want is what matter is for. I am that I am, and the rest is women and the wilderness, to be used as I see fit ("Woman/Wilderness" 161).

This separation between man on the one hand, and woman and nature on the other, as its subordinates, is rooted in Christianity (Gunn Allen 245; Abram 94) and has incessantly worked its way into the Western psyche.

In historical terms, the bond between humanity and the natural world is suggested to have been damaged by Christianity's arrival, "destroying pagan animism" (White 10), which was the belief that "every tree, every spring, every stream, every hill had its own *genius loci*, its guardian spirit . . . Before one cut a tree, mined a mountain, or dammed a brook, it was important to placate the spirit in charge of that particular situation, and to keep it placated" (White 10). Nevertheless, "Christianity made it possible to exploit nature in a mood of indifference to the feelings of natural objects" (White 10). Thus, in opposition to a pre-Christian conception of the world in which humanity was subject to and in need of nature,

the notion that nature is somewhere over there while humanity is over here or that a great hierarchical ladder of being exists on which ground and trees occupy a very long rung, animals a slightly higher one, and man . . .—especially 'civilized' man– a very high one (Gunn Allen 246) gradually gained prominence, to the point of shaping a "universe ... primarily on a sense of separation and loss" (Gunn Allen 244). It is in this environment that human society finally diverts from the path of nature, becoming "a substance isolated from nature" (McDaniel 189) that possesses the divine power to rise above the laws of the natural world (White 10). As a consequence of this division, humanity's regard for its ecosystem will change drastically, since the latter will no longer hold any power with which to lure humankind (Helfland 48). Hence, the relationship between these two entities becomes one of exploitation and profit, supported by the representatives of Christianity itself, who claim that "nature has no reason for existence save to serve man" (White 14). The conception of the ecosystem as a warehouse that humanity is entitled access to for raw materials and provisions has reached our days, and Henry David Thoreau was one of many who denounced this paradigm change. Writing in the nineteenth century, Thoreau laments how, even though "husbandry was once a sacred art [nowadays] it is pursued with irreverent haste and heedlessness by us, our object being to have large farms and large crops merely" (155). This profit-oriented mindset seems to be what upsets Thoreau the most, and he claims that "by avarice and selfishness, and a grovelling habit, from which none of us is free, of regarding the soil as property, ... the landscape is deformed, husbandry is degraded with us, and the farmer leads the meanest of lives. He knows Nature but as a robber" (Thoreau 155). Although *Walden* (1854) was written almost two centuries ago, there is no denying that these words are still more than applicable to our current world.

Ursula Le Guin seeks to overthrow this long-established idea of a world made for man and his rule, where the whole of creation—including women and nature—are there for his use and profit. Since man's hegemony is a completely arbitrary construct, Christopher Manes suggests that it can and should be fought. In his words, " 'Man' is not an inevitability. He came into being at a specific time due to a complex series of intellectual and institutional mutations, among them the sudden centrality of reason. He could just as inexplicably vanish" (26). For this purpose, it is essential that we "challenge the humanistic backdrop that makes 'Man' possible, restoring us to the humbler status of *Homo sapiens*: one species among millions of other beautiful, terrible, fascinating—and signifying—forms" (Manes 26). In light of this, Le

Guin seeks to remove man from the central place granted him by the Judaeo-Christian myth of creation (Buell, *The Future of Environmental Criticism* 105), and force him to share a common space with the rest of beings in a universe whose existence depends on the forces of nature.

Although Earthsea is, as we are suggesting, a subversion of the Christian anthropocentric myth of creation, it is true that language is the spark that ignites the flame of life in both Christianity and Earthsea (Comoletti & Drout 116). In the same fashion as the Christian God brought the whole world and its inhabitants into being by command of His voice, so did Segoy animate the fictional world devised by Le Guin in its first stages, where "the beginning was the word" (Spivack 31). There is evidence of this in "The Creation of Éa", the poem about the origins of Earthsea:

> Before bright Éa was, before Segoy
> bade the islands be,
> the wind of dawn blew on the sea . . .
> Only in silence the word. (Le Guin, *Description* 390–391)

However, as Tom Shippey points out, this shared feature of the two creation myths should not be taken to diminish Le Guin's subversive goal. He writes that, although using and considering language's creative element, Le Guin did so "more seriously and more literally than . . . many other theologians" ("The Magic Art and the Evolution of Words: The Earthsea Trilogy" 117). So much so, that Shippey catalogues her as "a myth-breaker not a myth-maker" ("The Magic Art and the Evolution of Words" 117), her work "existing in defiance of twentieth-century orthodoxies, whether semantic, scientific, or religious" (Shippey "The Magic Art and the Evolution of Words107). Somewhat in line with Shippey's comments, Robert Scholes also shares the belief that Le Guin has gone beyond her Christian heritage, mainly due to the fact that her work's "perspective is broader than the Christian perspective—because finally it takes the world more seriously than the Judaeo-Christian tradition has ever allowed it to be taken" (36). This 'going-beyond' that Scholes suggests is a feature of Le Guin's work can be seen in, among other things, her treatment of death. In Le Guin's work, death is no longer a taboo, or the obscure issue it is in Christianity, but an essential part of the life of any being (Scholes 38), and to have a conception of life without death—and vice versa—would be impossible. In a similar manner to what Jonathan Bate suggests is Wallace Stevens's aim with his poem "Sunday Morning" (1915–1923), Le Guin is looking "to put aside the immortal longings of the old religion … the ultimate end of which is to conquer space and time, to master weather, to stop the clock which counts us to our death" (115).

We may here talk of how the place of the American West granted Le Guin the opportunity to carry out the subversion of Christian anthropocentrism discussed above. Frederick Turner was a defender of the idea that America was, on the whole, naturally suited to create its own mythology. He writes that "We do not need to accept our myth of nature and culture. The state of America is the state of being able to change our myths" (48). Martin Simonson and Raúl Montero Gilete argue that the West, in particular, is a geographical and social space especially appropriate for the creation of new legends that, although rooted in European tradition, are adapted to this new environment (29). Setting off from this premise, they later on embark on a study of the new American hero that emerged in North American literature, for whom it is essential to develop a relationship of interaction and worship with the natural world in which he is thrust (Simonson & Gilete 31), where nature, due to the ecological conditions proper to the West, becomes chaotic and violent (Simonson & Gilete 32). This hero finally evolves into a figure that, veering away from his European roots, becomes one with the American environment (Simonson & Gilete 37) acquiring knowledge from it, due to the intimate relationship developed between the two (Simonson & Gilete 38). This shows us how these new stories will develop a character of their own, a rather regional one, even though the root from which they have originally stemmed is European, just as Le Guin proposes in her *Earthsea* saga. In her case, we have seen how one of the pillars around which she constructs her fantasy universe is the will to displace a religion arriving in America from Europe as was Christianity; an intentionally executed relegation that, still, will not prevent her from incorporating some of its elements into her own myth, as the centrality of the spoken word.

What, then, is Le Guin's newly-devised ecocentric universe like? As an author that "works with an ecology" (Scholes 37), the particularity of her work resides in "its naturalism, its reverence for the balance of life, and its refusal of transcendental values" (Slusser 83). We could say these three characteristics are Earthsea's founding features: nature's centrality, the need not to disturb the natural balance of the cosmos, and the thought that no individual is entitled to transgress nature's limitations. This world view coincides with Michel Serres's condition, set in his work *The Natural Contract* (1992), for a more appropriate relationship between humanity and nature. According to Serres, "we must indeed place things at the center and us at the periphery, or better still, things all around and us within them like parasites" (33). In addition, Le Guin's proposal orbits in equal measure around Lawrence Buell's take on environmental ethics, namely "that the interest of the ecosphere must override that of the interest of individual species" (*The Future of Environmental Criticism* 137).

Humanity's role within this specific cosmos does not allow it to claim any ownership of said world, although human individuals are given a certain degree of authority in Earthsea, in that they have the ability and the power to shape and affect the world, although they remain subjects to its everlasting forces. In a sense, this is "an authority without supremacy—a non-dominating authority" (Le Guin, "Bryn Mawr Commencement Address" 148), which Le Guin attributes to the peculiar mindset of the Native American. Indeed, her naturalistic conception of Earthsea could be said to share several similarities with the Native American relation to nature. It is not our purpose here to claim that Le Guin's thoughts on human–nature relationship were directly borrowed from Native American culture, but we would like to suggest that there may exist an affinity between the two. For instance, nature is central to the Native American understanding of the world. As Navajo Scott Momaday states,

> from the time the Indian first set foot on this continent . . . he has centered his life in the natural world. He is deeply invested in the earth, committed to it both in his consciousness and his instinct. In him the sense of place is paramount. Only in reference to the earth can he persist in his true identity (qtd. in Reed 28).

Given the essential place that nature occupies in the Native American psyche, it is little wonder that they come to "[assume] that the earth is alive in the same sense that human beings are alive" (Gunn Allen 256), permeated with that "unit of consciousness [that] is the All Spirit" (Gunn Allen 257). Additionally, nature showcases religious or spiritual attributes, as "a source of divine revelation" (Reed 29) and as can be seen in its application to totemism (A. Kroeber 837). Native American culture also displays belief in a necessary equilibrium of the cosmos, stemming from a conception of the whole range of beings that inhabit the world as lacking hierarchy. This includes "[acknowledging] the essential harmony of all things and [seeing] all things as being of equal value in the scheme of things, denying ... opposition, dualism, and isolation" (Gunn Allen 243), together with "[allowing] all animals, vegetables, and minerals ... the same or even greater privileges than humans" (Gunn Allen 243).

Nature's centrality and depiction in Earthsea may also bring animism to mind. Animism is "the sense of an all-pervasive spiritual power in nature" (Hughes 7), which leads the individual "to a feeling that one ought not to injure the living things that share the world with mankind, or alter the natural arrangement even of land and sea, because nature is divine" (Hughes 7). This reminds us of those places in Earthsea where the Old Powers of the Earth seem to be still present, and which humans need to approach with respect and reverence, since their anger can be devastating. Places like the Tombs of Atuan, the Immanent Grove, Roke Knoll, and the cave at Aurun are all places that almost seem to have a life of their own. As pointed out above, animism seems to have come to an end with the arrival of Christianity, leading to "the natural world [losing] its numinosity, its sacredness" (Hughes 21) and the consequent blind exploitation of nature on behalf of human civilisation (Hughes 22). This adds yet more relevance to Le Guin's ambition to subvert the Christian paradigm.

One last idea that we would like to mention about Earthsea's complexion is the unity formed by each of its several forces and inhabitants. This shows connotations of what Jonathan Bate refers to as

> the relatively new science of ecology, which emphasizes the interconnectedness of all things. [This model] shows us the wholeness of the living globe, shows us 'the extreme intricacy and precision of its interconnected working parts—winds, currents, rocks, plants, animals, weathers, in all their swarming and law-abiding variety' (27–28).

Isaiah Berlin's simile on this issue is worth considering, when he writes that "the world can be conceived organically—like a tree, in which every part lives for every other part, and through every other part" (5), where everything partakes in "the eternal all-containing spirit" (Berlin 20). In fact, Crow and Erlich refer to Le Guin as "a firm proponent of the oneness of the world" (200), which is to say that Earthsea, "[a] world of land and sea . . . is Le Guin's concrete image for the idea that all things—organic and inorganic, material and spiritual, object and force—shape and are shaped by each other" (Cummins 10). There are a few scholarly works addressing the existence of this particular conception of the universe in Le Guin's work, pointing to diverse sources of inspiration ranging from medieval times (Tsai 150) to Emerson's proposals (Rochelle, *Communities of the Heart. The Rhetoric of Myth in the Fiction of Ursula K. Le Guin* 113). We should also mention the presence of this belief in Native American culture. In this regard, Paula Gunn Allen writes about their widespread conviction that "all of life is living—that is, dynamic and aware, partaking as it does in the life of the All Spirit and contributing as it does to the continuing life of that same Great Mystery" (243). Le Guin herself praises the Native American assumption of the human being as part of a supreme apparatus—something that the European colonisers did not embrace. She writes how

> what the Whites perceived as a wilderness to be 'tamed' was in fact better known to human beings than it has ever been since: known and named. Every hill, every valley, creek, canyon, gulch, gully, draw, point, cliff, bluff, beach, bend, good-sized boulder, and tree of any character had its name, its place in the order of things. An order was perceived, of which the invaders were entirely ignorant. Each of those names named, not a goal, not a place to get to, but a place where one is: a center of the world. ("A Non-Euclidean View of California as a Cold Place to Be" 82)

Earthsea may also be said to be very akin to yet another image of the world as one sole unit, namely "the Gaia hypothesis, the idea that the whole earth is a single vast, living, breathing, ecosystem" (Bate 146). Devised by James Lovelock and developed in detail in his book *Gaia: A New Look at Life on Earth* (1979), this theory proposes that "the entire range of living matter on Earth, from whales to viruses, and from oaks to algae, could be regarded as constituting a single living entity" (Lovelock 9), where "important environmental properties . . . have to be kept in subtle balance if life is to persist" (Lovelock 16).

Indeed, the need for a persisting balance expressed by Lovelock is paramount for the welfare of Le Guin's fictional world. In Earthsea, "the principle that sustains being is the Equilibrium" (Crow & Erlich 221), which is similar to Lovelock's propositions of a "near-infinity of creatures performing essential co-operative tasks" (44) that calls for an "intricate system of check and balances" (Lovelock 46). This Equilibrium implies that every agent in said fictional world fulfils a crucial role, even those forces that seem as opposite as "light and darkness" (Le Guin, *AWoE* 199), and the powers of good and evil (Bucknall 47). This necessary measured cooperation between antagonists appears to be a crucial condition for life in Earthsea, even as it was at its moment of genesis, as told in "The Creation of Éa":

> Only in silence the word,
> only in dark the light,
> only in dying life. (Le Guin, *Description* 391)

The inhabitants of Earthsea are perfectly aware of this arrangement, as can be perceived in Ged's words: "There is no end. The word must be heard in silence. There must be darkness to see the stars. The dance is always danced above the hollow place, above the terrible abyss" (Le Guin, *TFS* 543). This balance should not, however, be thought of as an immutable being, since "a wizard's power ... can shake [it]" (Le Guin, *AWoE* 56). Ged's advice to Arren—who later becomes Prince Lebannen—is clarifying here:

> Do you see, Arren, how an act is not, as young men think, like a rock that one picks up and throws, and it hits or misses, and that's the end of it. When that rock is lifted the earth is lighter, the hand that bears it heavier. When it is thrown the circuits of the stars respond, and where it strikes or falls the universe is changed. On every act the balance of the whole depends. (Le Guin, *TFS* 477)

Hence, although changeable, the universe will always find a way, by means of lesser or greater adjustments, to keep the Equilibrium, so that "the pattern [holds]" (Le Guin, *The Finder* 97).

This mandatory collaboration between opposite forces relates to the second requisite for Earthsea's proper functioning: the cycle of life, the never-ending process of life and death (Crow & Erlich 201). Regardless of our cultural conception of these as opposites, in Earthsea, death is but a precondition for life, and "to deny death is to turn from life" (Slusser 74). The necessity of death and its regenerative power is also implicit in Lovelock's conception of Gaia, as when he says that "it is so often ignored or deliberately forgotten that the unending death-roll of all creatures, including ourselves, is the essential complement to the unceasing renewal of life" (125). Again, it is Ged who shows the greatest sensibility for this issue, claiming that "only what is mortal bears life ... Only in death is there rebirth. The Balance is not a stillness. It is a movement—an eternal becoming" (Le Guin, *TFS* 562). This becoming hints at the idea of death as a contribution to the organic world, fusing with "the earth and sunlight, the leaves of trees, the eagle's flight ... And all who ever died, live; they are reborn, and have no end, nor will there be an end" (Le Guin, *TFS* 613). "The Creation of Éa" is also clear on this idea of "[returning] forever to the source" (Le Guin, *Tehanu* 860):

> The making from the unmaking,
> the ending from the beginning,
> who shall know surely?
> What we know is the doorway between them
> that we enter departing. (Le Guin, *Description* 392)

The above paragraphs have aimed to show how Le Guin's conception of Earthsea drinks from different cultural springs. Setting off from a Christian tradition that she wants to displace, although borrowing from it the centrality of the spoken word in the creation of her universe, she moves towards more ecocentric conceptions of the cosmos, which implies that her work combines both tendencies. Tonia Payne writes that Le Guin and Thoreau shared a similar objective, namely that of being able to offer their compatriots a new cultural standpoint from which to understand their own land (52). This implied combining the best of European and Native American cultures to produce a hybrid that suited the new world, which is what Simonson and Montero Gilete suggest happened in the American literature of the West around the nineteenth century. Applying their ideas to Le Guin's work, we could say that Earthsea's myth of creation, and the parameters that it sets, can be thought of as another example of Le Guin's aforementioned goal, since she has been able to create a universe that shares, among other elements, the Native's relationship with the natural world, based on knowledge, sensibility and spirituality, while also making responsible applications of European social institutions (Simonson & Montero Gilete 33).

The central role of nature in Earthsea gives it enormous and extraordinary powers, some of them, as has been suggested, used in the very creation of said world. Throughout the different stories that comprise Le Guin's saga, nature is portrayed as an entity of strong character. Before commenting on what conception of nature is featured in these stories, it would be interesting to learn what their author has to say about it. Le Guin states explicitly that she could not conceive of a nature that is "warm, comfortable, and easy" ("Ursula Le Guin" 10), believing this to be a rather "simplistic" view ("An Interview with Ursula K. Le Guin" [Freedman] 46). This is the type of nature that Garrard calls "unsullied purity" (195). On the contrary, she admitted to preferring "things a little dirty and messy. Mixed up. Mucky" ("An Interview with Ursula K. Le Guin" [Freedman] 46). Le Guin thus devised her conception of nature as ambivalent, possessing "light and darkness" (Crow & Erlich 201) within itself. As Ged puts it: "The Earth is beautiful, and bright, and kindly, but that is not all. The Earth is also terrible, and dark, and cruel. The rabbit shrieks dying in the green meadows. The mountains clench their great hands full of hidden fire" (Le Guin, *TToA* 347). This, nonetheless, should not lead us to think of nature as either good or evil. As pointed out above, in the case of the dragons, nature also escapes the grasp of human tags. Instead, nature in Earthsea needs to be regarded as "pre-ethical" (Le Guin, *Description* 412), and, using George Slusser's words, any attempt to categorise it as evil is nothing less than "a misunderstanding of the dynamics of life" (74).

We find exponents of this ambivalent nature all across Earthsea, although two stand out: the so-called Old Powers and the places where they are manifest, and the dragons. These, in turn, can be divided into two principal categories: those that portray nature's darkest and most dangerous, even destructive, character, and the ones representing its most pleasant face. It is interesting to see how this dualist view of the natural world, in addition to the influence of the West's environment, may also reflect Le Guin's Taoist beliefs, more precisely the yang-yin symbol, which represents the light and dark of every being.

As for the representatives of a darker nature, we have mentioned the dragons and the Old Powers. Since the former have already been studied in detail above, we shall only focus on the latter. These powers of nature are tremendous (Le Guin, *AWoE* 142), omnipresent (Le Guin, *TOW* 218), and uncontrollable (Le Guin, *The Finder* 116), "bound each to an isle, a certain place, cave or stone or welling spring" (Le Guin, *The Finder* 148). Thus, they can be found in places like "Roke Knoll, the Immanent Grove, the Tombs of Atuan, the Terrenon [and] the Lips of Paor" (Le Guin, *Description* 391). While among these spots where the Old Powers are manifest there are some, like the Lips of Paor, that do not clearly fall into either of the opposite categories of Earthsea's ambivalent nature, there are others that can definitely be considered to belong to either its darker or brighter side. For instance, the Terrenon and the Tombs of Atuan fall into the dark and destructive category. The former is a stone "made when the world itself was made, and will endure until the end of the world" (Le Guin, *AwoE* 138), in which "an old and terrible spirit was imprisoned" (Le Guin, *AwoE* 138). The particular quality of this stone is the knowledge that it can grant to the person that touches it (Le Guin, *AwoE* 142). However, it is also said to carry "great evil" (Le Guin, *AwoE* 139), perhaps the very same peril inherent in a limitless knowledge, which, as we shall see below, is a central issue in Le Guin's work. The Tombs of Atuan, on the other hand, are home to the Nameless Ones, which are, to an extent, portrayed as evil spirits. The spirits residing in the Tombs make them a treacherous (Le Guin, *TToA* 276) and "deathly place" (Le Guin, *TToA* 344), although they are simultaneously able to create some of the most beautiful sights humans can behold. These spirits were able to produce a

> great vaulted cavern beneath the Tombstones . . . jewelled with crystals and ornamented with pinnacles and filigrees of white limestone[;] . . . immense, with glittering roof and walls, sparkling, delicate, intricate, a palace of diamonds, a house of amethyst and crystal, from which the ancient darkness had been driven out by glory (Le Guin, *TToA* 291).

Power, then, although destructive, also has the ability to trigger beauty. Such is the force of the Old Powers that, driven by anger, they tear down the Tombs and the place where they were worshipped—a destruction that they survive (Le Guin, *TToA* 338). Thus, the Terrenon and the Tombs of Atuan—together with the dragons whenever these showcase their most aggressive character, hint at a specific facet of nature, which is its wildest, most dangerous (Garrard 68), even destructive aspect, ready "[to take things] away from us" (Serres 36).

In contrast, Earthsea is also home to some very tranquil and beautiful landscapes, even if the Old Powers are present in some of them. Such a place, where humans and the forces of nature live in a rather relaxed relationship is the Isle of Roke, which is "the heart of Earthsea" (Le Guin, *The Finder* 84) and epicentre of magic in said archipelago, due to, among other things, it being the location of the school of magic. On this isle, there are a couple of spots where nature is most present. The first of them is Roke Knoll, a promontory that "was the first that stood above the sea, when the First Word [of creation] was spoken" (Le Guin, *TFS* 419). If one stands on top of it, its connections with nature are easily felt, "the roots of it . . . deep, deeper than the sea, reaching down even to the old, blind, secret fires at the world's core" (Le Guin, *AWoE* 74). Another place that displays an extremely tight bond with the natural powers is the Immanent Grove. This enchanted forest is "the heart of peace" (Le Guin, *TOW* 218), and, although unpredictable (Le Guin, *Dragonfly* 339), a place of truth (Le Guin, *Dragonfly* 338) and beauty. According to Ged, the

> leaves [there] don't all turn in autumn, but some at every season, so the foliage is always green with a gold light in it. Even in a dark day those trees seem to hold some sunlight. And in the night, it's never quite dark under them. There's a kind of glimmer in the leaves, like moonlight or starlight (Le Guin, *TOW* 214).

However, the crucial element in the Immanent Grove is none of those just mentioned. Its most important characteristic appears to be its centrality to the very life of Earthsea, as it is considered its heart (Le Guin, *TOW* 36). It is the static axis around which the rest of life moves (Le Guin, *TFS* 409), the soil where "the roots of knowledge" (Le Guin, *The Finder* 84) lie deep. It is so essential to Earthsea's wellbeing and correct functioning that,

> if ever the trees should die so shall [wizards'] wisdom die, and in those days the waters will rise and drown the islands of Earthsea which Segoy raised from the deeps in the time before myth, all the lands where men and dragons dwell (Le Guin, *AWoE* 89).

Regarding areas that stand out not due to their connection with the power of nature, but thanks to their natural beauty and tranquillity, we can count Selidor and Gont. The way these lands are depicted can remind the reader of the landscapes of "Eden, Paradise, the Golden Age, and the idyllic garden" (Kolodny 6). Selidor is an area of Earthsea where dragons can be found in their natural habitat. Its description reads as follows:

> The dunes ran inland, low and grassy, for half a mile or so, and then there were lagoons, thick with sedge and saltreeds, and beyond those, low hills lay yellow-brown and empty out of sight. Beautiful and desolate was Selidor. Nowhere on it was there any mark of man, his work or habitation. There were no beasts to be seen, and the reed-filled lakes bore no flocks of gulls or wild geese or any bird. (Le Guin, *TFS* 587)

While Selidor, regardless of its beauty, may even seem slightly awe-inspiring due to its vast sceneries—Gont, and especially the area Re Albi—are the very definition of an idyllic, pastoral landscape (Sawyer 402). In this land, which is Ged's own birthplace, human society and nature have come to develop an exemplary relationship based on rational exploitation and stewardship. Even away from home, Ged's attachment to Gont brings memories of

> bright pools in the River Ar; . . . of Ten Alders village under the great slanting forests of the mountain; of the shadows of morning across the dusty village street, the fire leaping under bellows-blast in the smith's melting-pit in a winter afternoon, the witch's dark fragrant hut where the air was heavy with smoke and wreathing spells (Le Guin, *AWoE* 86).

Of course, no pastoral is such without the presence of "shepherds[,] . . . cow- and goatherds" (Garrard 39), which is also an essential economic activity in Gont.

On the whole, we can see how Le Guin devised an Earthsea that seemed to feature ideas put forth by several different philosophers and anthropologists. For instance, this fictional universe was originally a place where nature is at the centre and "behaves as a subject" (Serres 36), creating and shaping that world. As has also been shown, humanity, belonging to the original dragon-human race that inhabited the archipelago, was meant to live on peaceful and responsible terms with nature, of which it was part. Thus, and drawing, to an extent, from diverse native cultures, Le Guin depicted a type of humanity that spoke nature's language (Abram 87), was meant to live according to the "rhythm learned from nature" (T. Kroeber & Heizer 92) and unfold a "sensitive, responsible environmental ethic" (Reed 26). However, putting theory into practice is not always easy, and if the responsibility of carrying that out falls into humanity's hands, it can certainly be even more difficult. Humankind's response to such a duty was the event of the Vedurnan, driven by a desire for dominance, using violence if need be. Its consequences, although originally related to other issues, can be found in the work of Horkheimer and Adorno: "the estrangement of human beings from the dominated objects" (21), namely dragons, and, consequently, nature itself. This alienation from the natural roots is what leads to the foundation of human society in Earthsea, which can reflect what has historically been considered a "move from the state of nature to that of civility [that can be] likened to the fall of man" (Bate 16). From here, humanity will come to regard the natural world that it inhabits "not as a potential 'home' in which to dwell" (McDaniel 197), but "as an 'other' to be manipulated and transcended" (McDaniel 197). Ultimately, the only worth given to nature will be that "of its instrumental value to human ends, rather than . . . its intrinsic value, that is, its value in and for itself" (McDaniel 201). This turn in the human attitude to nature can be clearly perceived in Earthsea in the evolution of two issues, both of them studied above: the change in the religious paradigm, from worship of nature to worship of the human; and humanity's loss of, and consequent need to, learn the Language of the Making, the language nature speaks in Earthsea. This new scenario brings about the steady degradation of human knowledge and society, for "ecocide and genocide go hand in hand" (Bate 64).

Nature and the Language of the Making

The deterioration of human–nature relationships in Earthsea—due to colonialist ambitions and the consequent alienation between the two—is portrayed with precision via different uses of magic. Before turning to the particular cases of Cob and Ged—examples of bad and good approaches to magic and knowledge, respectively—it is worth lingering, for a while, on the two factors that make wizardry possible in Earthsea: nature, and the Language of the Making.

The magic performed by the wizards and its sources form a kind of chain in which each link is connected to the one that comes before. We have previously shown how magic is directly connected to True Speech, and the magic power that each individual can achieve is also linked to, among other things, their knowledge of this original language. At the same time, the Language of the Making is deeply rooted in nature, as it is its own language, the very source of its existence. Highlighting the tight bond between nature and language, David Abram comments on how "the complexity of human language is related to the complexity of the earthly ecology—not to any complexity of our species considered apart from that matrix" (86). Abram also quotes fellow phenomenologist Merleau-Ponty, who referred to language as "the very voice of the trees, the waves, and the forests" (86). In the same way that nature is infinite, there seems to be "no end to that language" (Le Guin, *AWoE* 60) in Earthsea. According to Shippey, the way that names are afforded such importance in Le Guin's work is yet another sign of her ecocentric view: "In her imagined world, the devotion to the word rather than the thing is bound up with an attitude of respect for all parts of creation" ("The Magic Art and the Evolution of Words" 104). In making use of a language that is so rooted in nature, then, "the weaving of spells is itself interwoven with the earth and the water, the winds, the fall of light, of the place where it is cast" (Le Guin, *TFS* 483). In addition, what type of magic can be performed seems to depend on the local natural conditions of the place where the individual is performing it (Le Guin, *AWoE* 189).

The main reason that this language is so pivotal for wizardry, or "naming magic" ("Entretien" 144) as Le Guin calls it, is the peculiarity of the names that form it, that is, that they are conveyors of the being (Shippey, "The Magic Art and the Evolution of Words" 116) and the essence of that which they name (Le Guin, "Interview" 63). At the same time, the person that utters the name gains knowledge about the named entity, as "to know the true name is to know the thing" (Le Guin, "Dreams Must Explain Themselves" 9). The Language of the Making contains not only the true names of every object or phenomenon in the natural world, but also those given to humans when they come of age. This is perhaps the most important rite of passage from childhood to adulthood, since the individual will receive their true name, which will be different from the use-name that they have had until then (Le Guin, *AWoE* 21). Of course, this implies that the true being of humans is equally conveyed in their received true names. One scene is particularly clarifying on this issue. Having escaped the Tombs of Atuan, Ged and Tenar arrive in a city in the Kargish Lands. Not wanting the city guard to recognise him, Ged uses a spell that completely changes his appearance. Although this initially startles Tenar, when she utters the name Ged, the spell loses power and fades away from her perception and she is able to recognise the apparent stranger next to her (Le Guin, *TToA* 379).

Knowledge and power are two factors that appear to be frequently entwined (Le Guin, "Non-Euclidean View" 97), here exemplified by magic and True Speech. David Abram explains, in general terms, this relationship between language and power—or, in the case of Earthsea, magic—and how the latter can be obtained from knowledge of the former, writing that

> to assemble the letters that make up the name of a thing, in the correct order, was precisely to effect a magic, to establish a new kind of influence over that entity, to summon it forth! To spell, to correctly arrange the letters to form a name or a phrase, seemed thus at the same time to cast a spell, to exert a new and lasting power over the things spelled. (133)

Indeed, one of the most negative aspects of wizardry is the fact that, due to its deep knowledge of the natural world granted by the study of the Language of the Making, humans develop a false notion that they are elevated to a position in which they can claim mastery on anything (Le Guin, "Coming Back From the Silence" 96), even nature itself, to the point of being able to "[hold] it on a fine, thin leash, tightening it on [its] throat" (Le Guin, *AWoE* 112). The idea of language as a means to control our surroundings is not a new one (Payne 56–57; 120), and the issue of humanity's use of language to control and dominate nature has already been tackled in several studies on Le Guin's *Earthsea* cycle, from Tonya Payne's remark that "who owns the names owns the things" (115) to Deirdre C. Byrne suggesting how Le Guin "shows naming as a linguistic imposition, aimed at domesticating and controlling the Otherness of natural phenomena" (62). This power, granted to human society by the very language of creation, can ultimately lead to the modification of the natural world (Le Guin, "Telling Is Listening" 199). From here, it follows that, since "names ... validate, even perhaps confer existence" (Payne 55), giving something a new name translates into reshaping its being (Le Guin, *AWoE* 67).

As mentioned above, after the Vedurnan, humans gave up their knowledge of the Language of the Making in favour of the mastery of other crafts, and this meant that humans were eventually forced to learn that language again. This has been interpreted as quite a clear sign of human society's estrangement from nature. We would here like to suggest that the very event of True Speech being given that linguistic status in human society further enhances their alienation from the natural world. Philosophers have historically aimed to portray humanity as "*uniquely* unique; that our noble gifts set us definitively apart from, and above, the rest of the animate world" (Abram 77), and some have considered human language the differential factor setting us apart, while others look at it as the ultimate "symptom of humankind's apartness from other species and our consequent power to destabilize ecosystems" (Bate 149). Jonathan White's take on language is clarifying here:

> we become so enamored of our language and its ability to describe the world that we create a false and irresponsible separation. We use language as a device for distancing. Somebody who is genuinely living in their ecosystem wouldn't have a word for it (qtd. in Payne 335).

This is precisely the issue with humanity in Earthsea, it no longer forming an intrinsic part of their being, they need to reconfigure that arcane, natural knowledge in the shape of the Language of the Making.

Prior to the division between dragons and humans, this knowledge was inherent to all the inhabitants of Earthsea. As something that was innate to that primeval race, there was no urge to objectify it into an extant body. However, the human need and ambition to recover that lost knowledge made it necessary to shape it into a language as we know it today, for the survival and learning of which writing becomes essential (Le Guin, *Description* 384), with its endless lists of names compiled by the Master Namer and learned by anyone who aspires to become a wizard. This issue of the written word is in itself a crucial element in the division that language creates between human society and their ecosystem. Contrary to oral cultures, whose "gestures and signs were seen

112

as the least mediated form of communication, and therefore closest to nature, and their absence of syntax and abstraction seemed to guarantee an immediacy and honesty" (Murray 17), the creation of "the Greek 'alphabet', [led to] ... the progressive abstraction of linguistic meaning from the enveloping life-world" (Abram 102). This development enabled language to "[become] a ponderable presence in its own right" (Abram 107) and to bring humanity under its alluring spell. The illusion's deceit would consist of the idea that "the written letters bring not wisdom but only 'the conceit of wisdom', making men seem to know much when in fact they know little" (Abram 113), at the same time as it triggered a "more detached, abstract mode of thinking" (Abram 109). We are thus able to see how, although originally rooted in nature itself, we have, in a way, perverted this knowledge in that its use has been deprived of its essential and original connection with the living world. As Greg Garrard comments, "communications technologies, capable of infinite replication and wide dissemination of information, *have initiated a world of simulation, that now functions to supplant the real world*" (190, our italics).

Regarding the alienating effect of language, we should consider the implications of humanity's use of True Speech in Earthsea. We have previously mentioned how Le Guin herself categorised wizardry as something close to science, due to its inquisitive purpose (Tsai 149) and the fact that it "is developed with such precise and quasi-rigorous detail" (Freedman xvi). Many Le Guin scholars highlight and support this comparison, including Byrne (137) and Scholes (37), while others, although not categorising it as such, describe Le Guin's take on wizardry in terms that remind us of science. For instance, Shippey writes about wizardry's "intellectual" ("The Magic Art and the Evolution of Words"101) and "moral boundaries" ("The Magic Art and the Evolution of Words" 101) and Comoletti and Drout speak of True Speech's "ability to both describe the world perfectly and to change it" (120). If science can be considered to serve the purpose of a tool or the technological basis for some greater plan, such as obtaining knowledge on how something works and then make use of it, then its connotations become quite dark. Within the Romantic paradigm, the analytic scientific perspective was considered something akin to bringing death to the observed object (Berlin 114). In more scholarly terms, the deep knowledge of the ecosystem that science has given man

> [has] enabled him to modify and change the beings surrounding him, and by his
> experiments to interrogate nature with power, not simply as a scholar, passive and
> seeking only to understand her operations, but rather as a master, active with his
> own instruments (Sir Humphry Davy, qtd. in Bate 50).

All in all, what is clear is that, depending on the way it is used, wizardry combined with its most valuable tool, contain elements that can make it look like a means of domination, which can ultimately contribute to humanity losing contact with the ecosystem that it inhabits. Given the relationship that has just been established between magic and science, the following words by Payne can help us clarify this issue:

> Clearly science itself is not alienating. The sense that science has the only answer
> and that the scientist must remain separate from what is being observed leads to
> alienation; science that maintains the connection with the human and the cosmos
> is not only valuable but as true and as metaphoric, Le Guin suggests, as fiction
> (357).

As will be shown below, this is the factor that determines Ged and Cob's behaviour as wizards as either good or bad.

To anyone who considers making use of the power granted by wizardry, there are certain guidelines, or rules, to which one must adhere. The most important idea for wizards to bear in mind is that "their power was not theirs, but lent to them" (Le Guin, *Description* 412), which, at the same time, entails the notion that, as "a power greater than [their] own" (Le Guin, *TFS* 479), the greatest knowledge is "to know how to let it do" (Le Guin, *Dragonfly* 285), that is, not to meddle with its ways. The importance of being intensely aware of these factors resides in the fact that this power conveys "the wholeness of knowledge" (Le Guin, *The Finder* 71), which refers to its dualistic nature. This dualism necessarily conditions the way in which the individual should approach power, since it can serve either creative or destructive purposes, as conveyed in the following words, from Le Guin's *Dragonfly*: " 'If a word can heal, a word can wound,' the witch said. 'If a hand can kill, a hand can cure. It's a poor cart that goes only one direction" (298). This duality that is present within power, entailed in the idea that "danger must surround power as shadow does light" (Le Guin, *AWoE* 33), means that, if perverted by "fear or greed" (Le Guin, *The Finder* 14), "it [can] work great evil" (Le Guin, *AWoE* 154). The paradox of knowledge and the power drawn from it lies in the fact that, although essentially good, they can turn into pure evil if used in the wrong way.

Of course, the factor capable of corrupting power and directing it to evil is none other but our human selves. In the history of Earthsea, evil has been "a web ... men [have woven]" (Le Guin, *TFS* 411). This pessimistic view of humanity is traceable in the principal character in Le Guin's short story *The Finder*, Otter. He laments that

> there's an evil in us, in humankind. ... And everything we do finally serves evil, because that's what we are. Greed and cruelty. I look at the world, at the forests and the mountain here, the sky, and it's all right, as it should be. But we aren't. People aren't. We're wrong. We do wrong. No animal does wrong. How could they? But we can, and we do. And we never stop. (64)

In Taoism, we find the idea that every being and force in the universe contains the ability to create and destroy; it is what makes them what they are. In light of this, we should not blame the whole of humanity for every evil that has been done. Rather, we could say that it depends on the individual and their personal take on it (Le Guin, *The Finder* 9), as well as other complementary factors, like the presence of temptation (Le Guin, *On the High Marsh* 267), greed (Le Guin, *The Finder* 43), and ignorance (Le Guin, *The Finder* 101). It is this type of individual's "shoddy work that costs to mend" (Le Guin, *TOW* 46). John Crow and Richard Erlich neatly summarise this idea when they write that "evil comes with knowledge, with consciousness, and the birth of consciousness brings the knowledge of good and evil and the power to do each. Evil is the alliance of conscious knowledge with greed for life inherent in the unconscious" (214). Those who venture to tread this path risk tipping over into a humanly inherent ambition to dominate. As Le Guin suggests, "when [the power of those individuals] claims a privileged relationship to reality, it becomes dangerous and potentially destructive" ("Bryn Mawr" 149). However, as conscious individuals, a characteristic that is, at the same time, "our gift and our curse [all] we can do is be conscientious about it – do it rightly, not wrongly" (Le Guin, "Coming Back" 98).

Thus, apart from being conscious of what may be triggered by our individual approaches to power, we may also comment on other factors in the Earthsea world that may help us establish a wholesome relationship with power. Among these are characteristics like a lucid mind (Le Guin, *AWoE* 22) and a kind heart (Le Guin, *AWoE* 53). We may also mention the central idea that we need to stick to the root of power, which is where it maintains its purest and uncorrupted form. We have suggested how Earthsea's wizards draw their power from a language that stems from nature itself. Jonathan Bate's words may serve to clarify this thought, when he writes of our necessity "to live … with thoughtfulness and with attentiveness, an attunement to both words and the world, and so to acknowledge that, although we make sense of things by way of words, we do not live apart from the world" (23).

There are two more elements, central to Earthsea, that every wizard needs to take into account when making use of their power, namely the need to use power responsibly (Payne 122), and to be aware of the limitations that it demands (Tsai 149). Regarding the former, Crow and Erlich comment on the importance of universal considerations. They suggest that, given the effect that individual actions can have on the cosmos, "the decision to act should follow only after [the] consequences have been consciously examined and weighed against considerations of self" (208). In other words, universal welfare should always prevail over personal ambition. In fact, it is on such decisions that "our freedom" (Crow & Erlich 209) depends.

On the other hand, one of the teachings Ged learns from the Master Summoner is restraint:

> You thought, as a boy, that a mage is one who can do anything. So I thought, once. So did we all. And the truth is that as a man's real power grows and his knowledge widens, ever the way he can follow grows narrower: until at last he chooses nothing, but does only and wholly what he *must* do (Le Guin, *AWoE* 89).

Regarding our own world, Serres suggests that if power and the knowledge from where it comes are to be kept within boundaries, it is fundamental that they be based on reason (46). The same necessity applies in Earthsea. Here we again find the idea of the need to stay close to the root; the centre. If we expand our knowledge in a limitless way, we run the risk of disenchanting nature. This is precisely what Mark Twain advises us against in *Life on the Mississippi* (1883):

Now when I had mastered the language of this water and had come to know every trifling feature that bordered the great river as familiarly as I knew the letters of the alphabet, I had made a valuable acquisition. But I had lost something, too. I had lost something which could never be restored to me while I lived. All the grace, the beauty, the poetry had gone out of the majestic river! (qtd. in Sanders 189)

In Le Guin's fictional world, mage apprentices are taught that "that which gives [them] power to work magic, sets the limits of that power" (Le Guin, *AWoE* 60), and that, as a consequence, what matters most is to "do what is needed. And no more" (Le Guin, *TFS* 557). The necessity of responsible handling of limited power is also an idea the Transcendentalists promoted, with their critique of our ever-expanding knowledge, and is espoused by Taoism, as Tsai (150) and Bucknall (42) have suggested. Several examples can be found in the sacred book of the Tao, as in chapter 32:

To order, to govern,
is to begin naming;
when names proliferate
it's time to stop.
If you know when to stop
you're in no danger. (*Lao Tzu: Tao Te Ching: A Book about the Way and the Power of the Way* 43)

On the whole, the appropriate approach to power that Le Guin proposes in her *Earthsea* novels can be summarised in the natural contract outlined by Michel Serres. He speaks in favour of a relationship

of symbiosis and reciprocity in which our relationship to things would set aside mastery and possession in favor of admiring attention, reciprocity, contemplation, and respect; where knowledge would no longer imply property, nor action mastery … An armistice contract in the objective war, a contract of symbiosis, for a symbiont recognizes the host's rights, whereas a parasite—which is what we are now—condemns to death the one he pillages and inhabits, not realizing that in the long run he's condemning himself to death too. (38)

In the end, since our advancement as a society grants us knowledge and power that, at times, can be difficult to even believe to be true, "it is we who have the power to determine whether the earth will sing or be silent" (Bate 282).

Cob: Power That Dominates

In what is likely the clearest example of a completely wrong use of power, we will now turn to the character Cob—a powerful wizard featured in *The Farthest Shore*, the third book of the *Earthsea* series. After a brief introduction to his persona, we will try to throw some light on the reasons behind his transgressive behaviour, as well as the consequences it brings.

Under the influence of an unfathomable power, the wizard Cob was allured by the most dangerous uses of magic, such as the art of summoning. Making light use of this perilous art, he was challenged and punished by a young Ged, who, unfortunately, only managed to deter him from for a brief period of time (Le Guin, *TFS* 487–489). In the same way as Serres's proposed fallen humanity, Cob is fashioned as a wizard who has lost all "faculties of conscience, reason, and judgement" (94); has been led to avarice by wisdom (Le Guin, *TFS* 440) and caught up "in the struggle between the human desire to know nature, ... and the concomitant desire to master [it]" (Payne 3). This insatiable desire to know the secrets of life, "to know what comes next, [to have] it all mapped out" (Le Guin, "Non-Euclidean View" 97) clashes, as was briefly mentioned above, with Taoist and Transcendentalist teachings about the limits of wisdom. Regarding the latter, which arguably played an important role in the shaping of Le Guin's environmental ideas, we could bring up Margaret Fuller's words on science. She wrote that "by wild speculation and intemperate curiosity we violate [the Author's] will and incur dangerous, perhaps fatal, consequences" (129). The poem that works as a prologue to her *Summer on the Lakes, in 1843* (1844) expresses the need of restriction when it says that "I give you what I can, not what I would" (Fuller 2). Lao Tzu advocated in favour of a measured and restrained use of power, while warning against behaviour that did not heed this advice, with claims such as "The more ingenious the skillful [sic] are, / the more monstrous their inventions" (*Lao Tzu: Tao Te Ching* 74). It is precisely this that happens to Cob, who pays the price for the temerity of trying to outwit the laws of nature, a road that leads to nothing but annihilation. Lao Tzu's words may indicate that in Taoism there exists a relationship between the idea of humanity's alienation from nature and that of limitless knowledge and power, which, at the same time, is reflected in Earthsea.

Cob's loss of contact with the natural world can be said to be based on personal choice—a decision that becomes a desire to master its forces, as can be seen in the control that he exercises over several dragons (Le Guin, *TFS* 582). In order to subdue nature, Cob will employ all of his power in a quest that, applying Scott R. Sanders's own critique of humanity, could be catalogued as "reason's wholesale assault upon nature" (190). At the same time, this resembles humanity's "Faustian[,] ... arrogant, shocking, and suicidal disregard of [its] roots in the earth" (Fromm 39). His infraction resides in the search for immortality, "eternal life" (Le Guin, *TFS* 518), in response to "the self that cries *I want to live, let the world rot so long as I can live!*" (Le Guin, *TFS* 560, italics in original). Thus, he sets out to open a "wound" (Le Guin, *TFS* 429) through which one can travel between the realms of the living and the dead, a "dry, dark springhead, the mouth of dust, the place where a dead soul, crawling into earth and darkness, was born again dead" (Le Guin, *TFS* 617).

An interesting point of view from which to study the reasons that might have driven Cob to act the way he did is to interpret him as a herald of the Enlightenment.[36] Fashioned on the necessity of "liberating human beings from fear" (Horkheimer & Adorno 1), that fear of the unknown born from an irrational civilisation, the Enlightenment has been "understood in the widest sense as the advance of thought" (Horkheimer & Adorno 1). Figuratively speaking, the individuals that comprised this movement sought to cast some light on those issues that

---

36 Among the many characteristics of the Enlightenment, there are three that could be catalogued as foundational. First, we find the pivotal role granted to reason, on which "the way to truth lay" (Duignan, par. 4). Second, we could mention Locke's theory of the "social contract", which implies a change in Man from a natural state that guarantees the equality of every human being (Maltz & Maltz 47), to the creation of societies where men "[surrender] their freedom in exchange for the security of law and order" (Maltz & Maltz 46). Last, we have the central position that the social men of reason adopt and which "[installs] them as masters" (Horkheimer & Adorno 1). This dominant attitude covers individuals and nature alike. Regarding Le Guin's oeuvre, we will focus on this latter feature of the Enlightenment, since it is this that is most clearly present.

had until then been hidden under the darkness of unreason and super-stition. It is precisely this that Cob is after—the unveiling of one of the better-kept secrets of nature: the origin of life. Thus, in his quest for immortality, he must cast some light on the "deep ... springs of being, deeper than life, than death" (Le Guin, *TFS* 596). As pointed out above, this implies that he ultimately endeavours to bring nature and its forces under control, so as to make use of them. This idea of dominance is also conveyed by the presumptions of the Enlightenment, from the moment it postulated the superiority of the man of reason, especially of Euro-pean origin (Conrad 1005; Sardar xvi). From this lofty position, the rest of the world and its irrational and uncivilized inhabitants become, in a sense, the Other; mere objects at the European subject's hand. This is how Serres explains this Enlightenment belief:

> Mastery and possession: these are the master words launched by Descartes at the dawn of the scientific and technological age, when our Western reason went off to conquer the universe. We dominate and appropriate it ... Our fundamental rela-tionship with objects comes down to war and property (32).

At the same time, he mentions this predisposition to take possession of everything to have its origin in "the *libido dominandi* [which] is a never ending will to dominate, ... the incontestable mistress of universal his-tory" (58).

With this in mind, we could say that Enlightenment spreads its dom-ination across two major entities: on the one hand human cultures and civilisations that, from an Enlightenment point of view, are uncivilised and barbaric, and on the other, the natural world. As for the former, it is not clear at what point Enlightenment thinkers began to directly support and proclaim imperialist and colonialist ideas (Conrad 1006), though it is possible to establish a not-necessarily-direct cause-effect relationship between the two. Edward Said, in his work *Culture and Imperialism* (1993), comments on how, in Enlightenment circles across Europe, it was common to find voices on the issues of "the rights of native peoples and European abuses" (240) and in "opposition to slavery and colonial-ism" (Said 240). However, others, including Horkheimer and Adorno, perceive a clear connection between reason and domination, claiming that "Enlightenment is totalitarian" (4), since "imperialism [is] reason in its most terrible form" (Horkheimer & Adorno 70). Along these lines,

Sebastian Conrad mentions the need to understand expansionist consequences of the Enlightenment as "tied to conditions of globality: as a specific way of incorporating the world in the context of expansion of European trade relations, the annexation of military and commercial bases and colonies, and the cartographic mapping of the globe" (1010). This idea of universalism is also one from which postcolonialist scholars approach the Enlightenment. Due to the expansionist ambition that it gave birth to, they see the age of reason "not as emancipation but as deprivation" (Conrad 1006). This may, at the same time, have happened due to the fact that "it was only a small step . . . between positing universal standards and deciding to intervene and to implement those standards, also by force, under the auspices of a paternalistic civilizing mission" (Conrad 1006). In addition, the Enlightenment drove non-European nations to embrace Western ways and join the global economic system (Conrad 1016). One, historically widely used, ideological tool for the justification of imperialism is to degrade those whom one wants to master, which is where racism comes into play. Enlightenment thinkers were also guilty of engaging in discourse that positioned the master against ethnic and cultural minorities, as Voltaire did with the Jews and people of African origin (Poliakov 56), the latter being "constructed not as a real person with real history but an image" (Sardar xiv). Other thinkers expressed a predisposition to conduct experiments with colonised people (Poliakov 58), or directly condemned the deterioration of the Western White race from continuous mixing with other, 'inferior', races (Poliakov 59).

In a sense, we could say that Cob, too, seeks to dominate others as a way to increase his power. We learn how he lures people with an offer of eternal life, in exchange for them surrendering their names and power to him (Le Guin, *TFS* 519). However, this promise is untrustworthy, since the immortality they are granted is nothing like that which they were told they would get, and they are instead turned into Cob's puppets, made to come "at his summoning . . . At his word they may return. At his bidding they may walk upon the hills of life, though they cannot stir a blade of grass" (Le Guin, *TFS* 594).

Enlightenment anthropocentrism implied that, once man's irrational beliefs were cast away, he was entitled to command the natural world and make use of it as he wished (Bate 77). Lynn White comments that "what people do about their ecology depends on what they think about themselves in relation to things around them" (9). Given the tyrannical elements of the Enlightenment paradigm (Horkheimer & Adorno 6), it is little wonder that it focuses on that "form of knowledge which … most effectively assists the subject in mastering nature" (Horkheimer & Adorno 65). Historically, it is from this moment on that it starts to make sense to address the ecosystem as a mere object, "the forest [becoming] a place neither of mystery nor sanctuary but rather something to be managed" (Bate 168), attributable to "the utilitarian judgement, the profit motive" (Bate 140) that dominates the Enlightenment mindset. David Abram summarises nature's transition from agent to commodity, and its relation to colonialism:

> Descartes's radical separation of the immaterial human mind from the wholly mechanical world of nature … [provided] a splendid rationalization for the vivisection experiments that soon began to proliferate, as well as for the steady plundering and despoilment of nonhuman nature in the New World and the other European colonies. (78)

This idea of nature as a clockwork mechanism, "Nature Methodiz'd" as Alexander Pope put it (qtd. in Berlin 32), takes shape in the instrumentalisation of nature, which responds to the human ambition to know about its functioning and then use that knowledge "to dominate wholly both it and human beings" (Horkheimer & Adorno 2).

This is precisely how Cob perceives nature: a store from which he can draw all the power he wants. Cob employs this power onto humans and nature alike, while he seeks to inflict change on the latter by attempting to achieve immortality. The use he makes of the power acquired from his knowledge of the Language of the Making presents different connotations. One is the fact that Cob perceives nature as an enemy that needs to be defeated lest it devours you, or, in his case, condemns him to inevitable death. This type of human attitude, according to Chaia Heller, derives from an excess of avarice, since "if we are not conscious of our own greed, then we will see nature as a greedy force from which we must continually steal in order to survive" (231). Driven by that blind faith in his condition of superior agent, the knowledgeable man does not hesitate "to interfere with the natural order of things" (Lovelock 107) and, consequently, neglects nature's intrinsic perfection (Berlin 33), trying instead to impose his own, which, in Cob's mind, is the promise of eternal life. On the other hand, this character turns around the relationship that True Speech holds with nature, as he manages to "bind the action of wizardry, [and] still the words of power" (Le Guin, *TFS* 424). Rather than a body of knowledge that exists in unison with the universe, True Speech now becomes an instrument aimed at perverting the very being from which it was fashioned, and, consequently, it almost "[unmakes] the world" (Le Guin, *TFS* 424). This attitude of Cob's is related to the Enlightenment mindset, as observed by Jonathan Bate when he writes,

> the ecological form of the dialectic of Enlightenment is this: Enlightenment's instrumentalization of nature frees mankind from the tyranny of nature (disease, famine), but its disenchantment from [sic] nature licenses the destruction of nature and hence of mankind. 'Men have always had to choose between their subjection to nature or the subjection of nature to the Self'. (78)

Again, this does nothing but increase the distance between Cob and the cosmos he was meant to live in cooperation with. Nonetheless, it is the inevitable aftermath of pretending to live a deathless life, the fact that "in the moment of ... transcendence, humankind seeks to become not so much 'the paragon of animals' as a Being beyond the animal" (Bate 181). The weakening of the human–nature bond is yet another consequence of Enlightenment's division between man—the sole subject-agent—and the rest of the universe as object (Garrard 68). One of the potential reasons behind this is that, in his use of the Language of the Making, Cob turns his back on its source, that is, nature. That language that loses touch with "the whole of the sensuous world that provides [its] deep structure" (Abram 85) is one that "has forgotten its expressive depths" (Abram 85), which ultimately leads to its speaking community withdrawing from active contemplation of and gentle engagement with the world it inhabits (Abram 85). Comoletti and Drout highlight a similar concern with language in Earthsea, suggesting that "the self-referential structure" (124) of Cob's take on language, which goes against "that relation between signifier and sig-nified [as] not arbitrary but grounded in a firm physical reality" (Como-letti & Drout 124), reflects "the falling, decaying world of *The Farthest Shore*" (Comoletti & Drout 124). We could also mention the idea that alienation is an inevitable side effect of knowledge, as James Lovelock proposed, attributing to Descartes's legacy the idea that "the conventional wisdom of a closed urban society becomes isolated from the natural world" (135). In *The Other Wind* (2001), Le Guin shows how those societies that shun more complex knowledge are better able to remain in touch with the earth to which they are attached (233).

Everything that has been said makes it clear what Cob's major transgression is. His mistake resides in bringing the cycle of life to a stop by trying to achieve a state of immortality. Of course, "to refuse death is to refuse life" (Le Guin, *TFS* 544), which is the reason why his transgression will put Earthsea's much-needed Equilibrium at risk. In his commitment to achieve immortality, Cob is betraying Emerson's principle of nature's "serene order [being] inviolable to [humans]" ("Nature" 43), as well as disrupting humanity's respectful relationship with its ecosystem. Here, Cob simply goes against what Edward Thomas deemed proper human behaviour towards nature, namely that

> mortals dwell in that they receive the sky as sky. They leave to the sun and the moon their journey, to the stars their courses, to the seasons their blessing and their inclemency; they do not turn night into day nor day into a harassed unrest (qtd. in Bate 275).

Cob is addressed as "the Unmaker" (Le Guin, *TFS* 591) in clear reference to his destruction of the main principle of life, which is that there should also be death. What leads him to act in this way is his belief that "[he is] a man, better than nature, above nature" (Le Guin, *TFS* 611), and that consequently he has no need to adhere to the rules that nature imposes on every other being. We might say that this is the attempt of one who, not adhering to the most basic principles of life, blindly strives to elude death and consequently loses both (Le Guin, *TFS* 613).

Although we have presented Cob as a man of the Enlightenment, his actions go against its principal banner of reason and rationality, indeed his domain lies "beyond all reason" (Le Guin, *TFS* 509). Cob's unreason stems from his foul use of the Language of the Making, which evokes the link between language and human alienation presented above. In this case we will consider an idea proposed by Le Guin, where she warns of arbitrary uses of language. According to her, it is the "words separated from experience for use as weapons ... [that] make the wound, the split between subject and object, exposing and exploiting the object but disguising and defending the subject" ("Bryn Mawr" 151). Cob's use of True Speech—the way he uses its words—is completely detached from the natural world from which they originate, which simultaneously allows him to direct his power against that source. He is thus able to open a wound between the worlds of the living and the dead in order to draw profit from it, which is unending life. As Le Guin indicates, Cob believes that his infraction should by no means turn back and punish him, as he is reassured by his power. However, what we later learn is that no one is free from actions that make the balance of the world tremble in such a way as Cob's temerity does. This is because, according to William Howarth, in the same way as in science, this character's quest for a deathless life would present "solutions that only generate new problems" (79). What Cob learns is that he is fatally locked into what he has done and that his powers will not suffice for him to escape this impasse. These are his words when Ged offers him help:

> No one can ever set me free. I opened the door between the worlds and cannot shut it. No one can shut it. It will never be shut again. It draws, it draws me. I must come back to it. I must go through it, and come back here, into the dust and cold and silence. It sucks at me and sucks at me. I cannot leave it. I cannot close it. It will suck all the light out of the world in the end. All the rivers will be like the Dry River. There is no power anywhere that can close the door I opened. (Le Guin, *TFS* 615)

Here, Cob clearly comes to the realisation that no one can defy the ultimate power of nature, and that if human wills and actions are taken too far, there is a risk that "greed [will put] out the sun" (Le Guin, *TOW* 227).

George Slusser mentions how Cob's actions, in the same way that they destroy his own self, have serious consequences for the whole of Earthsea (80). Thus, all across the archipelago his wrong is felt as if there was "some evil at work" (Le Guin, *TFS* 403), as if "the springs of wizardry [had] run dry" (Le Guin, *TFS* 404). This situation of unbalance was already felt by the wise of Roke before it began to take form. For instance, we read that the Master Changer looks through a stone and has a vision of the islands of Earthsea disappearing, and how "each time . . . more islands are gone, and the sea where they were is empty and unbroken, even as it was before the making" (Le Guin, *TFS* 566). Similarly, the Master Summoner tells of how he saw "the streams run dry, and the lips of the springs of water draw back. And underneath all was black and dry" (Le Guin, *TFS* 569), which is a signal of "the Unmaking" (Le Guin, *TFS* 569). At the same time as they are running out of magic powers, there is a general forgetting of the lore that allowed the inhabitants of Earthsea to keep in touch with their ecosystem, such as songs (Le Guin, *TFS* 551). We could say that all these signals hint at a deep change in the universe, almost a kind of apocalypse, as if "the unbalanced sea would overwhelm the islands where [people] perilously dwell, and in the old silence all voices and all names would be lost" (Le Guin, *AWoE* 60). After this, the world, as known thus far, would cease to exist. The Summoner clearly sees that the ongoing change is leading them "towards death" (Le Guin, *TFS* 569), while Ged expresses it in a yet darker tone. He feels the danger behind "[the] blight upon the lands. The arts of man forgotten. The singer tongueless. The eye blind. And then? A false king ruling. Ruling forever. And over the same subjects forever. No births; no new lives. No children" (Le Guin, *TFS* 561).

Michel Serres expresses the shadow of humanity and the universe's potential destruction brought about by Cob's ambition to master life, commenting that "through our mastery, we have become so much and so little masters of the Earth, that it once again threatens to master us in turn" (33). The implication of this statement, together with what has been related about Cob's transgression of the natural limits, sets the focus on the importance of individual actions, a deeply rooted belief in, for instance, several Native American cultures (Gunn Allen 260; Silko 267). Recalling the image of Earthsea as a body of interwoven elements conveys the idea that "the more closely the planet is interconnected, the less room any of its inhabitants has for manoeuvre" (Garrard 205). In other words, the fact that Cob pulls several strings in his quest for immortality disturbs the whole tapestry represented by Earthsea.

Fortunately for the human inhabitants of the archipelago, Earthsea is restored to a state in which the balance appears to again rule undisturbed. It is interesting to see that, in order for this to happen, nature itself intervenes. This can be seen in a scene in Le Guin's *The Farthest Shore*, when Ged and Arren arrive in Selidor in their quest for stopping Cob. Once they confront him, Cob makes use of his power to immobilize Ged and Arren, which is the precise moment when the dragon Orm Embar arrives flying. We read how

vast and fiery, the great body of the dragon came in one writhing leap, and plunged
down full force upon [Cob], so that [his] charmed steel blade entered into the dragon's mailed breast to its full length: but the man was born down under his weight
and crushed and burned (601).

Even though Cob remains alive, Orm Embar's sacrifice is enough to free
Ged and Arren from the wizard's spell and they are thus able to follow
him through a portal and "down into the dark" (Le Guin, *TFS* 602),
where they finally overcome Cob and heal the wound that he opened.
The fact that a dragon—a representative of nature—sacrifices its life so
that the whole of the universe can keep on living hints quite clearly at the
imperative need to uphold the cycle of life. The wheel that Cob managed
to bring to a stop is thus again put in motion by means of death. In other
words, nature sacrifices one of its parts so that the whole can keep on
living. Additionally, Orm Embar's behaviour also hints at the effect that
individual actions can exert on a greater scale, in his case—as opposed
to Cob—for the better.

Nonetheless, and going back to the issue of the apocalypse mentioned above, we could say that the catastrophe proposed by Le Guin
imitates what Garrard calls "a blank apocalypse: an eschaton without a
utopia to follow" (101). In *The Other Wind*, Le Guin's sequel to *The Farthest Shore*, we learn that Cob's transgression has still not been healed
several years later, which implies that Ged's efforts and complete waste
of power were insufficient (167).

In order to explain how Cob's mistake could not be wholly righted
through the efforts of Ged and nature, we need to go back, for a moment,
to the time of the Vedurnan. The area colonised by humans would later
be referred to as the Dry Land, "the boundary from death into life" (Le
Guin, *TFS* 624). In order to learn more about its vital implications, the
following excerpt is worth quoting in full length:

The [ancient humans] saw that the dragon's realm was ... outside of time, it may
be... and envying that freedom, they followed the dragon's way into the west
beyond the west ... A timeless realm, where the self might be forever. But not in
the body, as the dragons were. Only in spirit could men be there ... So they made
a wall which no living body could cross, neither man nor dragon. For they feared
the anger of the dragons. And their arts of naming laid a great net of spells upon
all the western lands, so that when the people of the islands die, they would come
to the west beyond the west and live there in the spirit forever.

But as the wall was built and the spell laid, the wind ceased to blow, within the wall. The sea withdrew. The springs ceased to run. The mountains of sunrise became the mountains of the night. Those that died came to a dark land, a dry land. (Le Guin, *TOW* 227)

The direct aftermath of this process was that humans altered their own cycle of life, so that, from that moment on, life could never again be renewed by death. Every dead human would depart from the lands of the living and, due to the cycle being stopped, would be forced to stay in the dreadful Dry Land forever. This seems as though humans changed the paradigm of death from an organic process that effects a return to the soil from which it has been born, to a particular state of the spirit, which remains isolated and helpless. This new situation contributes, again, to human society's alienation from its ecosystem, since we learn that it is only humans that ever-set foot on Dry Land. Meanwhile, the rest of the inhabitants of Earthsea continue to return to the source, "to rejoin the greater being of the world" (Le Guin, *TOW* 145). Regardless of the dire peril implied by crossing the wall built by the first humans (Le Guin, *TOW* 29), which established the division between the realms of the dead and the living, Cob tries to manipulate said wall for his own benefit. Again, what he is after is to "break down that wall" (Le Guin, *TOW* 228) in order to achieve the "bodiless, immortal self" (Le Guin, *TOW* 228). Thus, it seems that Cob's manipulation of the wall, adding to humanity's primal temerity, last long after his other wrongs have been mended.

Horkheimer and Adorno offer their views—set in a different context—on these attitudes present in certain human beings, and the inability of the dead to fulfil their life cycles. They claim that "any attempt to break the compulsion of nature by breaking nature only succumbs more deeply to that compulsion" (9). This idea is directly applicable to humanity's situation in Le Guin's saga. As we have just seen, many tried to escape nature's imposition of a limited lifetime by going against nature's laws; trying to cheat them. However, since they are consequently disqualified from being one with the earth, the only thing that they managed to achieve was to grant their dead a life of unrest, that is, a worse type of death. This disturbed balance between life and death is the angular piece in Le Guin's *The Other Wind*, which is made clear when certain characters become aware that it is the dead themselves that are unsuccessfully trying to tear down that wall that barred them from rest (20–21), yearning for "death. To be one with the earth again. To re-join it" (Le Guin, *TOW* 228).

At the end of this novel, the wall is at last destroyed by the unified power of dragons and humans, setting free the dead in the Dry Land, each individual turning into "a wisp of dust, a breath that shone an instant in the ever-brightening light" (Le Guin, *TOW* 239). However, we should remember that the world of Earthsea, although an organism that strives to keep itself in balance, is affected by the deeds of its inhabitants, and that many of these effects last forever. Thus, although still within the Equilibrium, Earthsea is constantly reshaped and changed. Even the fact that dead humans are at last allowed to be free does not imply that the breach that was made at the very beginning of their civilization has been overcome. Instead, we can presume that humans still turn into their spirit forms when they die, unlike the rest of the inhabitants of the archipelago, who are allowed to unite with the source of life—nature. As the Master Doorkeeper suggests: "I think maybe the division that was begun, and then betrayed, will be completed at last … The dragons will go free, and leave us here to the choice we made" (Le Guin, *TOW* 233).

Ged: Power that Complies

Directly in opposition to Cob we find Ged. Although we will be able to see how his approach to power was initially not the most appropriate, he evolves to display a much more correct use of his force. Ged, who in his later days would become a Dragonlord and Archmage, showcases an enormous power from a very early age. At the age of twelve he succeeds in expelling a group of warriors that were trying to raid his village. He accomplishes this by means of his innate power to make magic, by invoking a mist that confuses and leads the invaders astray, thus saving the whole island. The deed does not go unnoticed, but reaches the ears of Ogion, an extremely wise wizard that lives on the island in Re Albi, and who encourages Ged to become his apprentice. However, Ged's first contact with the world of wizardry does not go down well. Already from his days as Ogion's apprentice, he "hungered to learn, to gain power" (Le Guin, *AWoE* 26). The mistake that lies in this attitude towards knowledge and power resides in the fact that such behaviour makes it extremely difficult for the individual to stick to the limits set by his craft, as Cob's case clearly shows.

Indeed, Ged initially also sets foot down this path. For instance, when still in Gont under Ogion's supervision, he starts meddling with dangerous spells. Reading through some books that Ogion had purposefully not yet shown him, he unintentionally begins to cast a spell. Suddenly,

> a horror grew in him, seeming to hold him bound in his chair. He was cold. Looking over his shoulder he saw that something was crouching beside the closed door, a shapeless clot of shadow darker than the darkness. It seemed to reach out towards him, and to whisper, and to call to him in a whisper; but he could not understand the words (Le Guin, *AWoE* 32).

Although Ogion's power frees him from this presence, its memory remains in his mind, like when, entering the school of wizardry in Roke, he thinks that "a shadow followed him in at his heels" (Le Guin, *AWoE* 45). We may think that, thanks to such experiences, Ged will begin to behave reasonably, but this is not the case. Lured by the potential power that he could gather with the knowledge acquired at school, and coupled with an innate ability to learn, Ged's student time in Roke is characterised by two tendencies: pride and hatred. In order to prove himself better than his peers, his sole aim is to gather all the knowledge that he can. Thus, when he finds a match to his power in fellow student Jasper, he

> swore to himself to outdo his rival, and not in some mere illusion-match but in a test of power. He would prove himself, and humiliate Jasper. He would not let the fellow stand there looking down at him, graceful, disdainful, hateful (Le Guin, *AWoE* 57).

This is the beginning of a feud between Ged and Jasper (72), which will lead Ged to the greatest transgression of his life.

As a way to find out who of the two is the most powerful wizard, Jasper dares Ged to "summon up a spirit from the dead" (Le Guin, *AWoE* 74), which he accepts. Ged is to show his power on Roke

Knoll—a place said to store enormous power. The scene is portrayed in such a way as to give the reader the feeling that he is standing above nature itself, having all its powers under his command. It reads as follows: "Under his feet he felt the hillroots going down and down into the dark, and over his head he saw the dry, far fires of the stars. Between, all things were to his order, to command. He stood at the centre of the world" (Le Guin, *AWoE* 75). This may remind us of Cob taking the very same stand, in which he would also think of himself as the master of nature, rather than subjected to its powers, and thus entitled to make use of its force according to his own will. Due to the summoning going completely wrong, Ged creates

> a rent in the darkness of the earth and night, a ripping open of the fabric of the world. Through it blazed a terrible brightness. And through the bright misshapen breach clambered something like a clot of black shadow, quick and hideous, and it leaped straight out at Ged's face (Le Guin, *AWoE* 76).

Almost a shapeless being (Le Guin, *AWoE* 77), it "was not flesh, not alive, not spirit, unnamed, having no being but what he himself had given it—a terrible power outside the laws of the sunlit world" (Le Guin, *AWoE* 103). This being that Ged has set free is a threat to the Equilibrium of Earthsea (Le Guin, *AWoE* 82), which is one of the reasons it becomes "his task ... to finish what he [has] begun" (Le Guin, *AWoE* 177). The other, and main, reason is that, as he will later learn, the shadow is part of his own being, so that "it is bound to him" (Le Guin, *AWoE* 190). They are two sides of the same being. This is why the only way to finish with the threat of his shadow is for Ged to become one with it, which happens when both speak their true names, that is, 'Ged': "Aloud and clearly, breaking that old silence, Ged spoke the shadow's name, and in the same moment the shadow spoke without lips or tongue, saying the same word: 'Ged'. And the two voices were one in voice" (Le Guin, *AWoE* 213). This is the process by means of which Ged becomes

> whole: a man: who, knowing his whole true self, cannot be used or possessed by any power other than himself, and whose life therefore is lived for life's sake and never in the service of ruin, or pain, or hatred, or the dark (Le Guin, *AWoE* 216).

This, again, reminds us of that Taoist symbol of the yang-yin, hinting at the presence, cooperation, and balance of the opposite forces that exist in every being. Apart from being key to Ged's freedom as a complete human being, his balancing also contributes to keeping the universe in balance (Scholes 39), which, in turn, is a sign that, again, every "human being [is] a part of the Balance and to know that every human action will have impact, positive or negative, on other parts of the whole" (Tsai 158) is essential.

It is all these experiences and the basic, vital learnings that lead Ged to learn how to approach his power in order to make good use of it. In a sense, we see that he is following Ralph Waldo Emerson's belief that "life's continuum of experience . . . becomes . . . the basis of knowledge" (Rochelle, *Communities of the Heart* 112). Hence, in the following years until he wastes his power and forsakes the world of wizardry, Ged's use of his craft is marked by prudence, resorting to it only when it is most needed, to the point of, in Arren's words, being "miserly about employing his arts" (Le Guin, *TFS* 517). Having seen its potential consequences, Ged has clearly overcome any desire to claim his power over nature, and he would rather have it go its own way and for him to play by its rules. Quoting Michel Serres, he follows these ideas "because, unregulated, exceeding its purpose, counterproductive, pure mastery [turns] back on itself" (34).

During his time as Archmage, Ged was forced to fight Cob and the consequences of his transgression, as shown above. In order to close the rent opened by Cob, Ged sacrifices all of his power (Le Guin, *TFS* 619–620), effectively ending his days as a mage (Le Guin, *TFS* 630). It is also worth noting how, after mending Cob's wrong, Ged shows no resentment towards the fact that he has lost that which made him what he was, and he feels "not the least bitterness or regret" (Le Guin, *TFS* 626). Instead, he accepts that he did what was needed to preserve life. In a way, it is as if he blindly and remorselessly accepts adherence to the laws and rules imposed by nature, even if this implies personal sacrifice and damage.

Ged does not seek to go back to Roke as Archmage once his power is spent. Even though the Masters of the School ask him to do so, he feels he is not in the condition to remain in the world of wizardry. In other words, Ged chooses a simpler life of contemplation, or being, over the life of a wizard, which is based on doing. We learn that Ged has always been aware of the inconveniences, the risks, that the wizard lifestyle involves. Talking to Arren, he tells him the following:

> Try to choose carefully, Arren, when the great choices must be made. When I was young I had to choose between the life of being and the life of doing. And I leapt at the latter like a trout to a fly. But each deed you do, each act, binds you to itself and to its consequences, and makes you act again and yet again. Then very seldom do you come upon a space, a time like this, between act and act, when you may stop and simply be. Or wonder who, after all, you are. (Le Guin, *TFS* 439)

One of the things that we could say influence Ged to make such a decision is that, after so many years spent in the turmoil of a life of action, he needs to find who he really is. Another reason for Ged to set off in search of a life of being could be the attachment to nature he has felt throughout his life. Having seen that a mind like Cob's, which strives only for action, can be driven to exert both self- and world-destruction, Ged desires to return to the centre—to nature itself—so that he can be one with it again. This may happen due to the fact that he approaches nature, following Christopher Manes's description, as "alive and articulate" (15) in opposition to Cob, who regards it as a mere reserve of power. It could also be the case that Ged no longer agrees with the usage that wizardry makes of the Language of the Making; a type of knowledge that resembles science in the sense that it seeks to discern the laws and processes of nature in order to take advantage of them. In his study of Romanticism, Isaiah Berlin mentions how

> the only persons who have ever made sense of reality are those who understand that to try to circumscribe things, to try to nail them down, to try to describe them, no matter how scrupulously, is a vain task (140).

Ged, in refusing a world of wizardry that seeks nothing but profit from the natural world, has gone through this very experience, and he is now able to discern the real relationship that should exist between humanity and nature, which is one of communion.

Tonya Payne and Isaiah Berlin both affirm this idea of freedom achieved by acknowledging one's need to live in communion with the natural world, in Ged's case being "part of the pattern" (Le Guin, *The Finder* 72). In her study of Le Guin's work, Payne talks about the fact that "it is in the unadorned fact of human 'being' in the cosmos that value is found, in the human awareness of being part of something greater" (317). Again on the topic of Romanticism, Berlin comments that it is

> by identifying yourself with it, by creating with it, by throwing yourself into this great process, ... by identifying on the one hand spirit, on the other hand matter, by seeing the whole thing as a vast self-organising and self-creative process [that] [one] will at last be free (139).

Last, we could mention that this rejection of continuous action in favour of a more contemplative attitude has similarities with the teachings of the *Tao Te Ching* (Bucknall 62). According to Dena Bain, Ged arrives at a "state of Void or Quietness" (218) in which he "sees all becoming as one being" (Bain 221)—his persona but a mere element of the vast cosmos—by means of practising the wu wei. Ged is aware of the fact that each and every action carried out by every individual impact on the whole, so that "no one can achieve his aims by actions that create rhythmic oscillation between opposites" (Bain 213), which is precisely what his role of Archmage implied—being constantly caught in the battle between good and evil that served only to perpetuate the opposing sides. This is where this teaching of the Tao is called for, which can be described as "actionless activity" (Bain 213), that is, briefly explained, "an attitude rather than an act, state of being rather than doing" (Bain 213).

A second factor that shows us Ged's tight bond with the earth is the origin of his wizardry. All across Earthsea, there are variants of the art magic, many of them rooted in specific lands, such as the wizardry of Paln and the wizardry in Roke. Nonetheless, there is a yet more important division within magic, one that seems to even determine the type of wizard that the individual will become. This is the division between the power of wizards and the power of witches, which is to say the male and female variants. Of course, Le Guin's choice of words—the fact that she names her male magicians wizards and her female magicians witches—has its implications. While the male wizards are meant to embody wisdom, female witches apparently retain "the negative image of an ignorant woman who practices simple magic of herbal healing or even harmful black magic in the countryside" (Tsai 147). Within the *Earthsea* universe, women's practice of magic was regarded a "base craft" (Le Guin, *Description* 419), and since they were not allowed to learn words of True Speech, they spread and taught their knowledge only among themselves (Le Guin, *Description* 419–420). All this contributed to the bad reputation of their craft, even though it encompassed a very large range of diverse practices, such as "the care of pregnant beasts and women, birthing, teaching the songs and rites, the fertility and order of field and garden, the building and care of the house and its furniture, [or] the mining of ores and metals" (Le Guin, *The Finder* 5). This list makes clear that witches are attributed a close relationship with nature in Le Guin's work. According to Jonathan Bate, it is a common cultural practice to link women with "nature, with instinct and biology" (35). Contrasted to this we find the historical-cultural portrayal of men, and consequently of wizards in Earthsea, as a figure linked "with rationality and transcendence of nature" (Bate 35).

The reasonable wizards of Earthsea are, thanks to their exclusive study of the Language of the Making, also possessors of what, in their eyes, makes up true knowledge—the only one worthy of their consideration. As Horkheimer and Adorno point out, scientific knowledge—which, as we have seen—resembles that of wizards, is prone to "establish man as the master of nature" (1). This self-attributed elevated position has led wizards to adopt high self-regard and unlimited ambition, which has consequently turned them into a discordant note within Le Guin's universe. In fact, it is their greed that triggers the war in Earthsea, and war, in turn, is "a displaced male-generalized activity, something that men do and women don't" (Le Guin, "Ursula K. Le Guin's Life and Works: An Interview" 68). Since the dawn of the magical arts, wizards have frequently used their power when driven by pride and self-interest, their actions bringing disastrous social and ecological consequences (Le Guin, *The Finder* 4–5). Even those characters who act wrongly, many times seeking to make evil, are all male, like Cob, Thorion, a wizard called Gelluk, and, to a lesser degree, Ged himself. All in all, it is very clear how "it was men's ambitions . . . that had perverted all the arts to ends of gain" (Le Guin, *The Finder* 86).

Meanwhile, Earthsea's witches coexist with their ecosystem, which some would argue is also the case with women in the real world, who are marked by "the humility of dwelling" (Bate 150). Thus, instead of placing themselves on the top of a hierarchy, like wizards do, witches make it very clear that, for them, the earth comes first (Le Guin, *The*

Finder 116). In light of this, the connection between the natural world and women and their art is made very explicit, since, in addition to what has been said above, we also learn that their power was drawn from the raw force of the Old Powers (Le Guin, *Description* 411). This bond is highlighted by several Le Guin scholars, such as Warren Rochelle and Holly Littlefield. While Rochelle links women to dragons, even suggesting that they are the same being ("The Emersonian Choice" 422), Littlefield suggests that "a woman's knowledge ... is deeper and more connected to things outside her body" (255), to which she adds the example of Tenar. Here Littlefield focuses on Tenar's use of the Language of the Making, emphasising that it is presumably thanks to her condition as a woman that this language is second nature to her, men having more difficulty acquiring it (256). She concludes that Tenar cannot "force it into a language of control and domination" (256), since her relationship with nature is not hierarchical. To this we should include what Le Guin says about women. In her words, the most valuable contribution that women have made, and continue to make, to humanity is that of teaching "how to be human" (Le Guin, "What Women Know" 81), which may also explain the greater care for the earth that women usually display (Buell, *Writing for an Endangered World* 240). It could be the case that statements like those shown above lead people to think of Le Guin as a person who positions women above men, showcasing, in a way, some kind of reverse sexism. Although it is not the aim of the present study to identify Le Guin's feminist beliefs, we think that the positions outlined above answer not to a sexually biased mindset, but rather—as will be shown below—to concrete spiritual beliefs.

It is for all the above-mentioned reasons that women's power, although marginalised by a characteristically male hierarchy, appears to be stronger than that of men, being effective even when the power of wizards seems to be diminishing (Le Guin, *Dragonfly* 302). Here we may recall the words of Moss, a witch who lives close to Ged and Tenar in Gont. According to her,

> [women's] is only a little power, seems like, next to [men's] ... But it goes down deep. It's all roots. It's like an old blackberry thicket. And a wizard's power's like a fir tree, maybe, great and tall and grand, but it'll blow right down in a storm. Nothing kills a blackberry bramble (Le Guin, *Tehanu* 747).

Ged, although a man, is an heir to precisely this approach to magic, which, using Garrard's words, proposes "immersion rather than a confrontation" (84) with nature. This is because he is the last link in a chain of wizards whose first steps into the world of wizardry have been taken within the feminine branch (Crow & Erlich 202), as Ged's mentor Ogion was, in his own time, mentored by Heleth, himself apprentice to a witch called Ard (Le Guin, *The Bones of the Earth* 225–226). Hence, although having made mistakes in his youth, Ged has exactly that main feature characteristic of witch magic, namely being one with the source; with nature. Ogion is highly aware of his power's connection with nature, as well as of the fact that "his wizardry grew out of it" (Le Guin, *The Bones of the Earth* 207), and that, consequently, it should abide by nature's rules. It is presumably due to this feature that we read of the school of wizardry in Roke needing more Gontish wizards, since they acknowledge that they are missing something (Le Guin, *The Bones of the Earth* 210). This could explain why, some time later, wizards such as Cob or Thorion would come out of this school.

Since Ged is fashioned as a recipient of a female tradition, we could say that he is challenging the so-called "Myth of Man the Hunter" (Gruen 62), a picture of the male human that stems from the idea that it was "the act of killing . . . [that] established the superiority of man over animal" (Gruen 62). Shu Fen Tsai, commenting on the work of Sara Lefanu, writes that "in the Earthsea trilogy the ones with true power and wisdom are all men; women are either ignorant country women or petty witches playing low and black arts" (163). If to this we add the fact that, in the *Earthsea* saga, women are tightly linked to the natural world, which, in cultural terms, some deem to be a "particular patriarchal notion" (Gruen 77), it may seem that Le Guin did not hold her fellow women in particularly high regard. Nonetheless, we would like to argue that this is not the case. If women are portrayed as part of a patriarchal structure it is because the society of Earthsea is ruled by men, just like ours, which does not imply that Le Guin considered women to be inferior to men. Indeed, by what has been said in the paragraphs above we could state that her stance is entirely the opposite. Although witches are described as possessors of a lesser art, Le Guin presents women's power as the true one, and the few wizards who are in possession of it are portrayed as good and given considerable presence in her plots, like Ged and Ogion.

In addition, the idea that women are closer to the natural world may, in Le Guin, be imbued with Taoism, which regards women as possessors of the "yin, the soft, the dark, the weak, earth, water, the Mother, the Valley" (*Lao Tzu: Tao Te Ching* 119).

As a last idea, we would like to mention that Ged, in light of Serres's theory, can be interpreted as the perfect 'sage' of nature. This is, at least, what we can glimpse from his actions. For instance, being familiar with what unmeasured greed can bring, Ged advocates for "the demand for prudence" (Serres 93) to be present in wizards' use of their power. More importantly, as we have just seen he is

> well-versed in the natural sciences of the inanimate and the living … traveler in nature and society; lover of rivers, sands, winds, seas, and mountains; walker over the whole earth; … humanist and scientist, … green and seasoned, audacious and prudent; further removed from power than any possible legislator, … great, perhaps, but of the common people; … knowing and valuing ignorance as much as the sciences, old-wives' tales more than concepts, … [and] finally, above all, burning with love for the Earth and humanity. (Serres 94)

Conclusions

Throughout these pages, we have been able to discern two main directions in Le Guin's representation of nature. On the one hand, the chain of influence, reaching back to the European tradition and the genre of epic fantasy established by J.R.R. Tolkien, is clearly visible in Le Guin's choice of a pseudo-medieval setting, and her portrayal of a feudalized culture, where a central power that oversteps its bounds in relation to the natural world, finds clear precedents both in the Arthurian tradition and that of Tolkien. On the other hand, Le Guin's distinctively Western American context prompts a twist to the overarching plot-scheme of the old narratives: the old dream of a paradise in the West has been forfeited, but there is still room for hope—and by recognizing that the enemy is found at the very centre of our own culture, and that it is our own displacement from nature that has caused the rupture, the peripheral vision of previously neglected minorities are brought to the forefront in Le Guin's work.

In fact, we could say that the aforementioned ideas are interconnected. To start with, Le Guin's view of humanity as the destabilising element within a system of extremely intimate and intricate connections is made manifest. It is perhaps because of this that she so eagerly seeks to rid man of his centrality, which can be seen in her choice of creating a universe where, forsaking her religious European roots (Christianity), nature now sits at the very centre as the force that makes, unmakes, and rules, while humanity depends upon it.

Of course, for such an enterprise, it is essential that Le Guin grants a voice of their own to other identities, individualities or cultures that had remained silenced until then. Such an attempt is easily perceived in how she fashions this new universe of Earthsea by, in a sense, borrowing scores of characteristics and beliefs that have been shown to be prominent in cultures like that of the Native Americans or philosophies such as Taoism. This attitude of bringing to the centre those who had previously stood in the margins is the direct result of Le Guin's Western American context and her personal response to it.

Here, we should first of all mention the impact of the Californian society upon the author and her works. As seen above, this was a society that had from its conception been determined by strong multicultural strands, with the presence of Native Americans and the gradual arrival of Europeans, Asians, African-Americans, and Mexicans. Of course, not all these groups achieved centrality in this society; many remained in the margins. Le Guin was highly aware of their situation, as can be seen in her participation in marches for social equality and against the Vietnam War, frequent in 1960s San Francisco and Berkeley. Further, Le Guin's familial environment was determined by a profound respect for and interest in ethnic variety, as her anthropologist parents constantly had guests of various origins and developed close relationships with some, such as Le Guin's "Indian" uncles. Le Guin was conscious of the double-sided quality of anthropology. She knew that, if used respectfully, it was essential to giving voice to the minorities that lacked a voice of their own, but it had historically been used as a tool that reinforced their marginalisation.

Nonetheless, it is still curious to see how, even stripped of its centrality, humanity will continue to be the factor that manages to turn the world upside down. We have seen how the reason behind the deep changes that Earthsea suffers has clear colonialist connotations: first, the ambition on behalf of humanity to separate themselves from their dragon relatives and, then, to conquer paradise, the land of the dragons west of the world, where immortality is supposed to reside.

Now, if we look at such an act of colonialism as a means by which humanity seeks to improve their situation, it follows that this could be equalled to progress and the advancement of society in our own world, always striving to make our lives easier and longer. To some extent, nature is displayed as antithetical to the idea of progress. Le Guin does, in a sense, inherit Tolkien's views that blind progress had negative social, cultural, and environmental consequences. However, unlike the latter's almost absolute rejection of progress, in some cases considering it to be purely evil, Le Guin believed that, if conducted correctly, it could be beneficial for human society, while she also wrote about the inherent benefits of science. She considered these matters to be inseparable from our own being, claiming them to be elements that have made us what we are today. Not only that, but she also defended the idea that progress and science are part of us and that each individual practitioner determines whether it falls into the category of good or of evil, as each of us has the ability and power to make good or evil; to build and to destroy. Le Guin proposes that, if twisted to serve evil purposes, progress showcases a feature of domination, the idea that it can provide our society with a power great enough to master the entire world. In her work, she portrays such an attitude in the figure of Cob and his use of the Language of the Making, as he employs it as a potential tool to gain power and, hence, spread one's dominion over others. As was seen in Cob's actions, the domination exercised by progress is not only spread towards other human individuals or societies, but, equally importantly, towards the natural world. In Le Guin's work, this is often presented as the result of a wrong take on magic, as it has the ability to both control and deeply alter the natural world. The concern for the destruction of nature in her works is related not only to her tight bond with the ecosystem of the American West, but also with certain activities of the U.S. as a nation, such as the ecological consequences of its role in the Vietnam War.

The direct aftermath of such an attitude towards nature is the gradual and fatal separation of humanity from the natural world. In Le Guin's fictional world, although it is her evil characters who showcase a higher degree of alienation due to their desire to dominate—an alienation which is, at the same time, enhanced by their actions—, the whole of humanity suffers from the same condition due to factors such as the Vedurnan and the Language of the Making. The human estrangement from its natural environment works simultaneously as the reason and consequence of humanity's attitude and behaviour.

This deteriorated relationship between human society and nature in Earthsea implies that such an idyllic situation of humanity fully immersed in and engaged with the environment, as shown in some British fantasy, is very seldom featured in Le Guin's fantasy cycle. In turn, she constructed a universe that had known an idyllic state of affairs where humans and nature were one only at the very beginning and for a very short span of time. In fact, by the time the *Earthsea* stories take place, it is clear that humanity has already opened a gap between itself and its ecosystem, for reasons detailed above. It could be reasonable to think that in the face of such a state of affairs, Le Guin should offer her characters, and ultimately her readers, some sort of a paradise where hope resided and an ideal life could be redeemed. This is, however, not the case with Le Guin. Instead of a paradise, what she offers us is hope and resilience.

Le Guin's Earthsea, regardless of the damage inflicted on it by human society, is a world that does not seem to change that much after the advent of progress. It is true that we are given hints about the world of wizardry and human society changing for the worse at the end of the saga, after the dragons depart forever. Nevertheless, life does not seem to change as much for the common people. Nor does the detrimental change to magic—an important tool by means of which humans keep in contact with nature—seem to affect the connection that people without any relation to the world of wizardry had with their environment. In a way, it is as if, after a period of fear and uncertainty, life carries on almost as before. We would like to suggest that this conception of life, where not even a wrong take on progress can shake people's existence too profoundly, is influenced by Taoism and its balancing forces of the yang-yin. The same happens with life in Earthsea. This is not a world that is going to change overnight, where dark and light are in an endless opposition. Rather, Earthsea is a body that keeps a constant balance, so that after a period when its darkest or most destructive forces have been prominent, the world itself will manage to return to a state of equilibrium by its own volition.

Unlike a world like, say, Tolkien's Middle-earth, where progress translates into the world losing part of its beauty and enchantment, as after the departure of the Elves at the end of the Third Age—which is exactly what makes the idea of there somewhere being a paradise so much needed—, Le Guin's universe requires none of this. In Earthsea there is no need for a paradise because there is no disruption of life or, even, beauty; nothing comes to an end as such. Rather, everything follows a clear pattern where change is constant, which makes the idea of a place beyond the world where a continuation of life is possible completely unnecessary.

As a final remark, we could say that Le Guin's depiction of a universe with such a sensible depiction of the natural world and where the bond between nature and humanity is deeply altered, served a very precise purpose. In light of this, we could validate Tonya Payne's words, when she suggests that Le Guin was the person who took up Thoreau's torch in order to continue the latter's project of creating a new culture which, by taking the best of both European and American (Native and non-Native alike) culture, would guide the new generations of North Americans towards a life of complete integration in, and cooperation with, their environment. By taking bits and pieces from British fantasy literature and adding to these her own experiences as a Western American, Le Guin sought to create a legendarium that would help her fellow citizens lead simpler lives at their fullest in an ever-changing world.

Bibliography

Abram, David. *The Spell of the Sensuous*. New York: Vintage Books, 1996.

Abrams, M. H. *Natural Supernaturalism: Tradition and Revolution in Romantic Literature*. New York and London: Norton, 1973.

Alexander, Michael. "Introduction". *Beowulf: A Verse Translation*, Harmondsworth: Penguin, 1973, pp. 9–49.

Ansgar Kelly, Henry. "The Metamorphoses of the Eden Serpent During the Middle Ages and Renaissance." *Viator*, vol. 2, 1 Jan. 1971, pp. 301–28.

Ashley, Mike. *Algernon Blackwood: An Extraordinary Life*. New York: Carroll and Graf, 2001.

Attebery, Brian, *The Fantasy Tradition in American Literature: From Irving to LeGuin*, Bloomington, IN: Indiana University Press, 1980.

Ayers, Robert H. "Christian Realism and Environmental Ethics." *Religion and Environmental Crisis*, edited by Eugene C. Hargrove, University of Georgia Press, 1986, pp. 154–171.

Bain, Dena C. "The Tao Te Ching." *Ursula K. Le Guin*, edited by Harold Bloom. New York: Chelsea House Publishers, 1986, pp. 211–224.

Bate, Jonathan. *The Song of the Earth*. Cambridge: Picador, 2001.

Beer, Gillian, *The Romance* (first edition 1970), London: Methuen, 1977.

Berlin, Isaiah, *The Roots of Romanticism*. Princeton, NJ: Princeton University Press, 1999

Blackwood, Algernon, *Episodes Before Thirty*, New York: E.P. Dutton, 1923.

—. *Ancient Sorceries and Other Weird Stories*. London: Penguin Books, 2002.

Botting, Fred. *Gothic*. Abingdon & New York: Routledge, 2014.

Bucknall, Barbara J. *Ursula K. Le Guin*. New York: Ungar, 1981.

Buell, Lawrence. *The Future of Environmental Criticism: Environmental Crisis and Literary Imagination*. Hoboken: Blackwell Publishing, 2005.

—. *Writing For an Endangered World: Litearture, Culture, and Environment in the U.S. and Beyond.* Cambridge: Harvard University Press, 2001.

Bunce, Michael. *The Countryside Ideal: Anglo-American Images of Landscape.* London & New York: Routledge, 1994.

Burke, Jessica. "How Now, Spirit! Wither Wander You? Diminution: The Shakespearean Misconception and the Tolkienian Ideal of Faërie." *Tolkien and Shakespeare*, edited by Janet Brennan Croft. Jefferson, NC & London: Macfarland, 2007, pp. 25–41.

Byrne, Deirdre C. *Selves and Others: The Politics of Difference in the Writings of Ursula Kroeber Le Guin.* Pretoria: University of South Africa, PhD dissertation, 1995.

Campbell, Liam. *The Ecological Augury in the Works of J.R.R. Tolkien.* Zurich and Jena: Walking Tree Publishers, 2011

Carpenter, Humphrey, *J.R.R. Tolkien: A Biography* (first edition 1977) Boston & New York: Houghton Mifflin, 2000.

Clery, E.J. "Introduction", in *The Castle of Otranto* (first published 1764), by Horace Walpole, Oxford: Oxford University Press, 1998, vii-xxxiii.

Coleridge, Samuel Taylor, *Biographia Literaria* (first published 1817), Oxford: Oxford University Press, 1965.

Comoletti, Laura B. and Michael D.C. Drout. "How They Do Things with Words: Language, Power, Gender, and the Priestly Wizards of Ursula K. Le Guin's Earthsea Books." *Children's Literature*, vol. 29, 2001, pp. 113–141.

Conrad, Sebastian. "Enlightenment in Global History: A Historiographical Critique." *American Historical Review*, Oct. 2012, pp. 999–1027.

Cooper, Jean C. *Taoism: The Way of the Mystic.* Aquarian Press, 1972.

Cossío, Andoni. "Tree and forest models in Victorian/Edwardian fantasy: MacDonald, Morris and Grahame as Triggers of J.R.R. Tolkien's Creativity". London: CRC Press, 2020, pp. 411–417.

Coverley, Merlin. *Psychogeography.* London: Pocket Essentials, 2010.

Crow, John H., and Richard D. Erlich. "Words of Binding: Patterns of Integration in the Earthsea Trilogy." *Ursula K. Le Guin*, edited by Joseph D. Olander & Martin H. Greenberg. New York: Taplinger Publishing Company, 1979, pp. 200–224.

Cummins, Elizabeth. *Understanding Ursula K. Le Guin.* Columbia: University of South Carolina Press, 1993.

Dickerson, Matthew, and Jonathan Evans. *Ents, Elves and Eriador: The Environmental Vision of J.R.R. Tolkien.* Lexington, KY: The University Press of Kentucky, 2006.

Duignan, Brian. "Enlightenment." *Encyclopaedia Britannica,* 29 March 2019, https://www.britannica.com/event/Enlightenment-European-history. Accessed 26 June 2019.

Dunsany, Lord. *The King of Elfland's Daughter.* London: Gollancz, 2001.

Eksteins, Modris. *Rites of Spring: The Great War and the Birth of the Modern Age* (first edition 1989), New York: Anchor Books, 1990.

Emerson, Ralph Waldo. *The Essential Writings of Ralph Waldo Emerson* (edited by Brooks Atkinson), New York: Modern Library, 2000.

—. "Nature." *Essays and Poems by Ralph Waldo Emerson,* edited by Peter Norberg. New York: Barnes & Noble Classics, 2004, pp. 7–49.

Flieger, Verlyn, *Splintered Light: Logos and Language in Tolkien's World* (revised edition, first edition 1983), Kent, OH, and London: The Kent State University Press, 2002.

—. "Faërie: Tolkien's Perilous Realm". *Tolkien: Maker of Middle-earth.* McIlwaine, Catherine. Oxford: Bodleian, 2018, pp. 35–44.

Ford, Andrew. *Homer: The Poetry of the Past.* Ithaca, NY: Cornell University Press, 1993.

Freedman, Carl. "Introduction". *Conversations with Ursula K. Le Guin,* edited by Carl Freedman. Jackson: University Press of Mississippi, 2008, pp. ix–xxii.

Fromm, Harold. "From Transcendence to Obsolence: A Route Map." *The Ecocriticism Reader: Landmarks in Literary Ecology,* edited by Cheryll Glotfelty and Harold Fromm. Athens: University of Gerogia Press, 1996, pp. 30–39.

Fuller, Margaret. *Summer on the Lakes in 1843.* Boston: Charles C. Little and James Brown, 1844.

Fussell, Paul. *The Great War and Modern Memory.* Oxford: Oxford University Press, 2000.

Garbowski, Christopher, *Recovery and Transcendence for the Contemporary Mythmaker: The Spiritual Dimension in the Works of J.R.R. Tolkien.* Zurich and Jena: Walking Tree Publishers, 2004.

Garrard, Greg. *Ecocriticism*. London & New York: Routledge, 2012.

Garth, John. *Tolkien and the Great War*. London: HarperCollins, 2004.

—. *The Worlds of J.R.R. Tolkien: The Places that Inspired Middle-earth*. London: Frances Lincoln, 2020.

Gilliver, Peter, et al., *The Ring of Words: Tolkien and the Oxford English Dictionary*, Oxford and New York: Oxford University Press, 2006.

Grahame, Kenneth. *The Wind in the Willows*. Dorking: Templar Publishing, 2007

Graves, Robert, *Good-bye to All That* (first published 1929, revised edition 1957), London: Penguin, 2000.

Gruen, Lori. "Dismantling Oppression: An Analysis of the Connection Between Women and Animals." *Ecofeminism: Women, Animals, Nature*, edited by Greta Gaard. Philadelphia: Temple University Press, 1993, pp. 60–90.

Gunn Allen, Paula. "The Sacred Hoop: A Contemporary Perspective." *The Ecocriticism Reader: Landmarks in Literary Ecology*, edited by Cheryll Glotfelty and Harold Fromm. Athens: University of Georgia Press, 1996, pp. 241–263.

Hainsworth, John. *The Idea of Epic*, Berkeley: University of California Press, 1991.

Hattersley, Roy. *The Edwardians*. London: Abacus, 2004.

Helfland, Jonathan. "The Earth Is the Lord's: Judaism and Environmental Ethics." *Religion and Environmental Crisis*, edited by Eugene C. Hargrove. Athens: University of Georgia Press, 1986, pp. 38–52.

Heller, Chaia. "For the Love of Nature: Ecology and the Cult of the Romantic." *Ecofeminism: Women, Animals, Nature*, edited by Greta Gaard. Philadephia: Temple University Press, 1993, pp. 219–242.

Hodges, Kenneth. "Reformed Dragons: *Bevis of Hampton*, Sir Thomas Malory's *Le Morte Darthur*, and Spenser's *Faerie Queene*." *Texas Studies in Literature and Language*, vol. 54, no. 1, 2012, pp. 110–131.

Hollis, Matthew. *Now All Roads Lead to France: The Last Years of Edward Thomas*. London: Faber and Faber, 2011.

Horkheimer, Max, and Theodor W. Adorno. *Dialectic of Enlightenment: Philosophical Fragments*. Translated by Edmund Jephcott. Stanford: Stanford University Press, 2002.

Howarth, William. "Some Principles of Ecocriticism." *The Ecocriticism Reader: Landmarks in Literary Ecology*, edited by Cheryll Glotfelty and Harold Fromm. Athens: University of Gerogia Press, 1996, pp. 69–91.

Hughes, Donald. "Pan: Environmental Ethics in Classical Polytheism." *Religion and Environmental Crisis*, edited by Eugene C. Hargrove. Athens: University of Georgia Press, 1986, pp. 7–24.

Hynes, Samuel. *The Edwardian Turn of Mind*. London: Pimlico, 1968.

Jeffers, Susan. *Arda Inhabited: Environmental Relationships in* The Lord of the Rings. Kent, OH: Kent State University Press, 2014.

Jewers, Caroline. *Chivalric Fiction and the History of the Novel*. Gainesville: University Press of Florida, 2000.

Joshi, S.T. "Introduction". *The White People and Other Weird Stories*. Arthur Machen. London: Penguin, 2011, pp. xi–xxiv.

—. *Unutterable Horror: A History of Supernatural Fiction* (vol. 2). New York: Hippocampus Press, 2014.

Kipling, Rudyard. *Puck of Pook's Hill*. London: Pan Macmillan, 2016.

Kolodny, Annette. *The Lay of the Land: Metaphor As Experiece and History in American Life and Letters*. Chapel Hill: University of North Carolina Press, 1975.

Kroeber, Alfred. *Handbook of the Indians of California*. New York: Dover Publications, 1976.

Kroeber, Theodora, and Robert Fleming Heizer. *Almost Ancestors: The First Californians*. San Francisco, New York & London: Sierra Club, 1968.

Kunzru, Hari. "Ursula Le Guin: 'Wizardry is artistry' ", interview with Ursula K. Le Guin. *The Guardian*, 20/11, 2014.

Landow, George, 'And the World Became Strange' in Schlobin R., (ed.), 1982, *The Aesthetics of Fantasy Literature and Art*, Indiana: University of Indiana Press. pp. 105–140.

Le Guin, Ursula K. "A Description of Earthsea." *Tales From Earthsea*. Boston & New York: Houghton Mifflin, 2012, pp. 377–423.

—. "An Interview with Ursula K. Le Guin." *Conversations with Ursula K. Le Guin*, edited by Carl Freedman. Jackson: University Press of Mississippi, 2008, pp. 26–46.

—. "An Interview with Ursula K. Le Guin." *Time*, 11 May 2009, http://techland.time.com/2009/05/11/an-interview-with-ursula-k-le-guin/. Accessed 10 Sept. 2018.

—. "A Non-Euclidean View of California as a Cold Place to Be." *Dancing at the Edge of the World*, edited by Ursula K. Le Guin. New York: Grove Press, 1989, pp. 80–100.

—. "A Wizard of Earthsea." *Earthsea: The First Four Books*. London: Puffin Books, 2016, pp. 7–218.

—. "Bryn Mawr Commencement Address." *Dancing at the Edge of the World*, edited by Ursula K. Le Guin. New York: Grove Press, 1989, pp. 147–160.

—. "Coming Back from the Silence." *Conversations with Ursula K. Le Guin*, edited by Carl Freedman. Jackson: University Press of Mississippi, 2008, pp. 92–101.

—. "Dragonfly." *Tales From Earthsea*. Boston & New York: Houghton Mifflin, 2012, pp. 278–375.

—. "Dreams Must Explain Themselves." *Dreams Must Explain Themselves*, edited by Ursula K. Le Guin. London: Gollancz, 2018, pp. 4–12.

—. *Earthsea Revisioned*. London: Green Bay Publications, 1993.

—. "Entretien avec Ursula K. Le Guin." *Conversations with Ursula K. Le Guin*, edited by Carl Freedman. Jackson: University Press of Mississippi, 2008, pp. 124–162.

—. *Lao Tzu: Tao Te Ching: A Book about the Way and the Power of the Way*. Boulder: Shambala Publications, 1977.

—. "On the High Marsh." *Tales From Earthsea*. Boston & New York: Houghton Mifflin, 2012, pp. 231–277.

—. Review of *Benediction*, by Kent Haruf. *Words are My Matter: Writings About Life and Books 2000–2016*, edited by Ursula K. Le Guin. Easthampton: Small Beer Press, 2016, pp. 230–232.

—. Review of *Ledoyt*, by Carol Emshwiller. *Words are My Matter: Writings About Life and Books 2000–2016*, edited by Ursula K. Le Guin. Easthampton: Small Beer Press, 2016, pp. 222–226.

—. "Tehanu." *Earthsea: The First Four Books*. London: Puffin Books, 2016, pp. 635–890.

—. "Telling Is Listening." *The Wave in the Mind*, edited by Ursula K. Le Guin. Boulder: Shambhala, 2004, pp. 185–205.

—. "The Bones of the Earth." *Tales From Earthsea*. Boston & New York: Houghton Mifflin, 2012, pp. 202–230.

—. "The Farthest Shore." *Earthsea: The First Four Books*. London: Puffin Books, 2016, pp. 395–634.

—. "The Finder." *Tales From Earthsea*. Boston & New York: Houghton Mifflin, 2012, pp. 1–152.

—. *The Other Wind*. London: Orion, 2012.

—. "The Tombs of Atuan". *Earthsea: The First Four Books*. London: Puffin Books, 2016, pp. 219–394.

—. *The Wave in the Mind: Talks and Essays on the Writer, the Reader, and the Imagination*. Boston: Shambala Press. (2004)

—. *Ursula K. Le Guin: Conversations on Writing with David Naimon*, by David Naimon. Portland, Oregon, & Brooklyn, New York: Tin House Books, 2018.

—. "Ursula K. Le Guin: Free Speech, Press Are 'Liberty in Action'." *Street Roots*, 29 Sept. 2017, https://news.streetroots.org/2017/09/29/ursula-k-le-guin-free-speech-press-are-liberty-action. Accessed 10 Sept. 2018.

—. "Ursula K. Le Guin's Life and Works: An Interview." *Conversations with Ursula K. Le Guin*, edited by Carl Freedman. Jackson: University Press of Mississippi, 2008, pp. 67–76.

—. "Ursula Le Guin." *Conversations with Ursula K. Le Guin*, edited by Carl Freedman. Jackson: University Press of Mississippi, 2008, pp. 3–11.

—. "What Women Know." *Words are My Matter: Writings About Life and Books 2000–2016*, edited by Ursula K. Le Guin. Easthampton: Small Beer Press, 2016, pp. 81–87.

—. "Woman/Wilderness." *Dancing at the Edge of the World*, edited by Ursula K. Le Guin. New York: Grove Press, 1989, pp. 161–164.

Lewis, Matthew Gregory. *The Monk. Gothic Horror: The Castle of Otranto and The Monk*. Edited by Raúl Montero. Portal Publishing: Berkeley, 2016.

Lewis-Stempel, John. *Where Poppies Blow: The British Soldier, Nature, The Great War*. London: Weidenfeld & Nicolson, 2016.

Littlefield, Holly. "Unlearning Patriarchy: Ursula Le Guin's Feminist Consciousness in 'The Tombs of Atuan and Tehanu'". Extrapolation, vol. 36, no. 3, 1995, pp. 244–258.

Lobdell, J. The World of the Rings: Language, Religion, and Adventure in Tolkien (revised edition; first edition 1981), Chicago and La Salle, IL: Open Court, 2004.

Longley, Edna. "Introduction". The Annotated Collected Poems, by Edward Thomas, edited by Edna Longley. Highgreen: Bloodaxe, 2008, pp. 11–27.

Lovelock, James. Gaia: A New Look at Life on Earth. Oxford, New York, Toronto & Melbourne: Oxford University Press, 1979.

The Mabinogion (translated by Sioned Davies). Oxford & New York: Oxford University Press, 2007.

MacDonald, George. Phantastes. Grand Rapids, MI: Eerdmans Publishing, 2000.

Machen, Arthur. Far Off Things. London: Martin Secker, 1922.

—. The Great God Pan and The Hill of Dreams. Ocean Shores, WA: Watchmaker, 2010.

—. The White People and Other Weird Stories. London: Penguin, 2011.

Maltz, Harold, and Miriam Maltz. The Enlightenment. Michigan: Greenhaven Press, 2005.

Manes, Christopher. "Nature and Silence." The Ecocriticism Reader: Landmarks in Literary Ecology, edited by Cheryll Glotfelty and Harold Fromm. Athens: University of Gerogia Press, 1996, pp. 15–29.

Manlove, Colin. The Impulse of Fantasy Literature, London and Basingstoke: Macmillan Press, 1983.

Mathews, Richard. Fantasy: The Liberation of Imagination (first edition 1997), New York: Routledge, 2002.

McDaniel, Jay. "Christianity and the Need for New Vision." Religion and Environmental Crisis, edited by Eugene C. Hargrove. Athens: University of Georgia Press, 1986, pp. 188–212.

Mehta, Hemant. "Is Christianity Beneficial or Harmful to Society?" Patheos, 21 Oct. 2014, https://friendlyatheist.patheos.com/2014/10/21/is-christianity-beneficial-or-harmful-to-society/. Accessed 26 June 2019.

Mirrlees, Hope. *Lud-in-the-Mist*. Gollancz: London, 2008.

Montero, Raúl (ed.). *Gothic Horror: The Castle of Otranto and The Monk*. Portal Publishing: Berkeley, 2016.

Morris, William. *The Well at the World's End*. Phoenix Mill: Allan Sutton, 1996.

—. *The Roots of the Mountains. More to William Morris: Two Books that Inspired J.R.R. Tolkien: The House of the Wolfings and The Roots of the Mountains*. Seattle: Inkling Books, 2003.

Murray, David. *Forked Tongues: Speech, Writing, and Representation in North American Indian Texts*. Bloomington & Indianapolis: Indiana University Press, 1991.

Parker, Peter. *Housman Country: Into the Heart of England*. London: Abacus, 2017.

Payne, Tonia L. *'A Heart That Watches and Receives': Ursula Le Guin and the American Nature-Writing Tradition*. New York: The City University of New York, PhD dissertation, 1999.

Poliakov, Léon. "Racism from the Enlightenment to the Age of Imperialism". *Racism and Colonialism: Essays on Ideology and Social Structure*, edited by Robert Ross, Springer, 2011, pp. 55–64.

Prince, Alison. *Kenneth Grahame: An Innocent in the Wild Wood*. London: Alison & Busby, 1994.

Reed, Gerard. "A Native American Environmental Ethic: A Homily on Black Elk." *Religion and Environmental Crisis*, edited by Eugene C. Hargrove. Athens: University of Georgia Press, 1986, pp. 25–37.

Regenbogen, Joe. *Questioning History: 16 Essential Questions That Will Deepen Your Understanding of the Past*. Wilmington: Vernon Press, 2016.

Rexroth, Kenneth. "Classics Revisited LXI: Parkman's History". *Saturday Review of Literature*, 24 February, 1968.

Robinson, David M. *Natural Life: Thoreau's Worldly Transcendentalism*, Ithaca and London: Cornell University Press, 2004.

Rochelle, Warren G. *Communities of the Heart. The Rhetoric of Myth in the Fiction of Ursula K. Le Guin*. Liverpool: Liverpool University Press, 2001.

—. "The Emersonian Choice: Connections Between Dragons and Humans in Le Guin's *Earthsea* Cycle." *Extrapolation*, Winter 2006, pp. 417–426.

Rosebury, Brian. *Tolkien: A Cultural Phenomenon* (revised and expanded edition, first edition 1992: *Tolkien: A Critical Assessment*), Houndmills: Palgrave, 2003.

Said, Edward W. *Culture and Imperialism.* New York: Vintage Books, 1994.

Sanders, Scott R. "Speaking a Word for Nature." *The Ecocriticism Reader: Landmarks in Literary Ecology*, edited by Cheryll Glotfelty and Harold Fromm. Athens: University of Georgia Press, 1996, pp. 182–195.

Sardar, Ziauddin. "Foreword to the 2008 edition". *Black Skin, White Masks*, by Frantz Fanon. London: Pluto Press, 2008, pp. vi–xx.

Sawyer, Andy. "Ursula Le Guin and the Pastoral Mode." *Extrapolation*, Winter 2006, pp. 396–416.

Schlobin, Roger (ed.). *The Aesthetics of Fantasy Literature and Art*, Indiana: University of Indiana Press, 1982.

Scholes, Robert. "The Good Witch of the West." *Ursula K. Le Guin*, edited by Harold Bloom. New York: Chelsea House Publishers, 1986, pp. 35–46.

Segura, Eduardo and Thomas Honegger (eds.), *Myth and magic: Art According to the Inklings*, Zurich & Jena: Walking Tree Publishers, 2006.

Serres, Michel. *The Natural Contract.* Translated by Elizabeth MacArthur and William Paulson. Ann Arbor: University of Michigan Press, 1995.

Shippey, Tom. "The Magic Art and the Evolution of Words: The Earthsea Trilogy." *Ursula K. Le Guin*, edited by Harold Bloom. New York: Chelsea House Publishers, 1986, pp. 99–117.

Shippey, Tom. *The Road to Middle-earth* (revised and expanded edition, first edition 1982), Boston and New York: Houghton Mifflin, 2003.

Silko, Leslie M. "Landscape, History, and the Pueblo Imagination." *The Ecocriticism Reader: Landmarks in Literary Ecology*, edited by Cheryll Glotfelty and Harold Fromm. Athens: University of Gerogia Press, 1996, pp. 264–275.

Simonson, Martin. "Recovering the Utterly Alien Land: Tolkien and Transcendentalism", in Segura, Eduardo and Thomas Honegger (eds.), *Myth and magic: Art According to the Inklings*, Zurich & Jena: Walking Tree Publishers, 2006, pp. 1–20.

—. *The Lord of the Rings and the Western Narrative Tradition*. Zurich and Jena: Walking Tree Publishers, 2008.

—. (ed.). *Representations of Nature in Middle-earth*. Zurich and Jena: Walking Tree Publishers, 2015.

—., and R.M. Gilete. *El Western fantástico de Stephen King: Hibridización y desencantamiento de la tradición literaria europea en* El Pistolero. Berne: Peter Lang, 2017.

—. "Out of this World: Tom Bombadil in Middle-earth". *Inklings Jahrbuch*, 35, 2018, pp. 143–156.

—. *El Oeste recuperado: La literatura del pasado y la construcción de personajes en* El Señor de los Anillos. Bern: Peter Lang, 2019

—. "The Final Frontier: Fictional Explorations of the Borders of Nature and Fantasy in Early Twentieth-Century Imaginative Literature". London: CRC Press, 2020, pp. 425–430

Slusser, George E. "The Earthsea Trilogy." *Ursula K. Le Guin*, edited by Harold Bloom. New York: Chelsea House Publishers, 1986, pp. 71–83.

Spivack, Charlotte. *Ursula K. Le Guin*. Boston: Twayne Publishers, 1984.

Stevens, John. *Medieval Romance: Themes and Approaches*, London: Hutchinson University Library, 1973.

Thomas, Edward. *The South Country*. London: Everyman, 1993.

—. *Rest and Unrest*. London: Duckworth, 1910.

Thomas, Helen, with Myfanwy Thomas. *Under Storm's Wing, Including As It Was and World Without End, Letters and Memoirs*. Manchester: Carcanet, 1997.

Thoreau, Henry David. *Walden*. London: Penguin Books, 2016.

Tolkien, J.R.R. *The Tolkien Reader*, New York: Ballantine Books, 1966.

—. *Sir Gawain and the Green Knight, Pearl, Sir Orfeo*. New York: Del Rey, 1975.

—. *The Lord of the Rings*. London: HarperCollins, 1993.

—. *Beowulf: A Translation and Commentary, with Sellic Spell*. London: HarperCollins, 2014.

—. *Smith of Wootton Major*. London: HarperCollins, 2015.

—. *The Story of Kullervo*. London: HarperCollins, 2015.

—. *The Letters of J.R.R. Tolkien* (edited by Humphrey Carpenter with the assistance of Christopher Tolkien, first edition 1981), Boston: Houghton Mifflin, 2000.

—. *The Return of the Shadow: The History of The Lord of the Rings* (Vol. 1, edited by Christopher Tolkien; first edition 1988). Boston and New York: Houghton Mifflin, 2000.

Trilling, Lionel and Harold Bloom (eds.). *Victorian Prose and Poetry*. New York, London, and Toronto: Oxford University Press, 1973.

Tsai, Shu Fen. "Le Guin's Earthsea Cycle: An Ecological Fale of 'Healing Wounds.'" *Concentric: Studies in English Literature and Linguistics*, Jan. 2003, pp. 143–174.

Turner, Frederick. "Cultivating the American Garden." *The Ecocriticism Reader: Landmarks in Literary Ecology*, edited by Cheryll Glotfelty and Harold Fromm. Athens: University of Gerogia Press, 1996, pp. 40–51.

Walpole, Horace. *The Castle of Otranto. Gothic Horror: The Castle of Otranto and The Monk,* edited by Raúl Montero. Portal Publishing: Berkeley, 2016.

White, Lynn Jr. "The Historical Roots of Our Ecologic Crisis." *The Ecocriticism Reader: Landmarks in Literary Ecology*, edited by Cheryll Glotfelty and Harold Fromm. Athens: University of Gerogia Press, 1996, pp. 3–14.

Williamson, Jamie. *The Evolution of Modern Fantasy: From Antiquarianism to the Ballantine Adult Fantasy Series*. Basingstoke and New York: Palgrave Macmillan, 2015.

Zaczek, Iain. *Fairy Art: Artists and Inspirations*. London: Flame Tree Publishing, 2005.

Zanger, Jules. "Heroic Fantasy and Social Reality". *The Aesthetics of Fantasy Literature and Art*, edited by Roger Schlobin. Indiana: University of Indiana Press, 1982, pp. 226–236.

*Critical Perspectives on English and American
Literature, Communication and Culture*

Edited by
María José Álvarez-Faedo, Andrew Monnickendam &
Beatriz Penas-Ibáñez

The peer-reviewed series provides a forum for first-class scholarship in the field of English and American Studies and focuses on English and American literature, drama, film, theatre and communication. The series welcomes critical perspectives on the reading and writing of texts, the production and consumption of high and low culture, the aesthetic and social implications of texts and communicative practices. It publishes monographs, collected papers, conference proceedings and critical editions. The languages of publication are both English and Spanish. Scholars are invited to submit their manuscripts to the editors or to the publisher.

Vol.   1   Juan Jesús Zaro
Shakespeare y sus traductores. Análisis crítico de siete traducciones españolas de obras de Shakespeare.
2007, 176 p. ISBN 978-3-03911-454-2

Vol.   2   María José Chivite de León
Echoes of History, Shadowed Identities.
Rewriting Alterity in J. M. Coetzee's *Foe* and
Marina Warner's *Indigo*.
2010, XVI, 241 p. ISBN 978-3-0343-0070-4

Vol.   3   Nela Bureu Ramos (ed.)
Flaming Embers.
Literary Testimonies on Ageing and Desire.
2010, 361 p. ISBN 978-3-0343-0438-2

Vol. 4   Manuel Brito
          Means Matter.
          Market Fructification of Innovative American Poetry in
          the Late 20th Century.
          2010, XII, 170 p. ISBN 978-3-0343-0444-3

Vol. 5   José Ruiz Mas
          Guardias civiles, bandoleros, gitanos, guerrilleros,
          contrabandistas, carabineros y turistas en
          la literatura inglesa contemporánea (1844–1994).
          2010, 395 p. ISBN 978-3-0343-0506-8

Vol. 6   Juan Ignacio Oliva (ed.)
          The Painful Chrysalis.
          Essays on Contemporary Cultural and Literary Identity.
          2011, 282 p. ISBN 978-3-0343-0666-9

Vol. 7   Celia M. Wallhead (ed.)
          Writers of the Spanish Civil War.
          The Testimony of their Auto/Biographies.
          2011, 329 p. ISBN 978-3-0343-0696-6

Vol. 8   Laura Ma Lojo Rodríguez
          Moving across a Century.
          Women's Short Fiction from Virginia Woolf to
          Ali Smith.
          2012, 131 p. ISBN 978-3-0343-1064-2

Vol. 9   Marta Sofía López
          Ginealogías sáficas.
          De Katherine Philips a Jeanette Winterson.
          2012, 167 p. ISBN 978-3-0343-1125-0

Vol. 10   Marta Fernández Morales (ed.)
          La década del miedo.
          Dramaturgias audiovisuales post-11 de septiembre.
          2013, 398 p. ISBN 978-3-0343-1311-7

Vol. 11   Michele Bottalico (ed.)
          No! In Whispers
          The Rhetoric of Dissent in American Writing
          2018, 240 p. ISBN 978-3-0343-2001-6